THE PARTRIDGES AT BAT

All eyes in the stadium were on Keith Partridge—except for his sister Laurie's. Laurie's eyes were fixed on Leo Rampkin, the broad shouldered curly-haired teacher who had a new interest in the Partridge family.

"Have your eyes always been blue, Leo?" she said.

But Leo wasn't paying much attention to Laurie. Keith had just come up to bat. There was a man on first and third. The pitcher released the ball and it zipped toward home plate on a blurred line . . .

Keith swung the bat with dizzying speed and then came the sound like no other in the entire history of the sports world! *Crack!*

And that's when it happened. That's when Keith, the rock idol became Keith, the hero!

D1483994

THE PARTRIDGE FAMILY #3

KEITH, THE HERO

BY MICHAEL AVALLONE

Based on a series created by Bernard Slade

CURTIS BOOKS

MODERN LITERARY EDITIONS PUBLISHING COMPANY
NEW YORK, N.Y.

For the Chilelli Family
—one and all.

Cast of characters . . .
and *not* in a pear tree.

SHIRLEY PARTRIDGE ... Mother
KEITH PARTRIDGE ..... Number One Son
LAURIE PARTRIDGE .... Number One Daughter
DANNY PARTRIDGE .... Number Two Son
CHRISTOPHER
     PARTRIDGE .... Number Three Son
TRACY PARTRIDGE .... Number Two Daughter
SIMONE .... Family Pet
REUBEN KINKAID ...... Manager

. . . and one psychedelic-colored, renovated old
school bus that takes them all over the country in
search of life, liberty and the pursuit of singing en-
gagements.

Table of Contents

Taped segment of the *America* Show, with master of ceremonies Clyde Clark interviewing Shirley Partridge of the sensational Partridge Family singing group . . .

CLARK: Hah hah, you sure are beautiful, Shirley. But tell us—I'm sure the audience would like to know—to what do you personally attribute the incredible success—there's just no other word for it—of the family?

SHIRLEY PARTRIDGE: Good health—and five children that sing like birds.

CLARK: Don't be modest, now. With all due respect, I'd say you were the brains of the outfit. The anchor man, you might say.

SHIRLEY PARTRIDGE: Not me. Anchors are a drag, aren't they?

CLARK: Will you be serious for one minute?

SHIRLEY PARTRIDGE: Oh, all right.

CLARK: Now, what would you really say has caused this immense success of yours as a singing group all over the country?

SHIRLEY PARTRIDGE: I wish I had a proper answer. All I know is we sing, the public buys our records, and they keep coming back for more. And asking us to come back. I guess if you were to pin it down to one thing, I'd have to say the kids are all with it, part of the *Now* scene—and that's the whole ball of wax. Okay?

CLARK: Okay.

At this point the interview was interrupted for a two-minute commercial, advertising *Crackly-Wackly* breakfast cereal . . .

1

TOO LONG AT THE FAIR

☐ Shirley Partridge gazed in despair at the sunburst clock on the living room wall. Despair transformed into a flare of anger. She controlled herself. After all, she was an adult, a mature, clear-thinking modern woman. It wasn't proper to give in to rage. Yet, she had five good reasons for losing her temper. And all of them were named Partridge.

The living room clock clearly showed that it was nearly six. And the kids should have been home over an hour ago. It wasn't like them to disobey her. Not like them at all—unless something unforeseen and unexpected had happened. She tried not to think about *that*. In a crowded lifetime that had seen her widowed and left with five growing children while she was still in her beautiful and lovely thirties, she was no stranger to tragedy. Nor to luck, either, for that matter. When she and her children had capitalized on their musical talent by recording a song in the garage behind the house and then watched that record hit the Top 40 and become a national best-seller, success had literally come to the Partridge Family overnight. Shirley Partridge, resourceful young widow, had seen her duty and had done it. She had abandoned her job as bank teller, bought an old school bus (which she and the kids personally painted in psychedelic hues) and the Partridge Family had become a barnstorming singing group which became a national fixture in no time at all. With a fine and shrewd manager like Reuben Kinkaid to steer them through Show Biz waters, the Partridges had enjoyed a startlingly successful career.

Still, Shirley was a mother first, a celebrity second.

And now it was six o'clock.

And Keith, Laurie, Danny, Christopher and Tracy Partridge were long overdue. Shirley had allowed them to attend the Meadowville County Fair that afternoon. She had begged off because there was too much to do around the house. For one thing, Reuben Kinkaid had signed them up for a two-week engagement at the fabulous Twilight Room in New York and the contract he had left on the kitchen table yesterday was worth going over a few times. And there were preparations to be made and phone calls to be made and a lot of those little important details that seem to be left to mothers only when a family is about to leave home for a few weeks.

Shirley hadn't minded letting the kids go without her. They were a good bunch and could take care of themselves. Keith and Laurie were in their teens, and though he was only ten, red-haired Danny Partridge was what Reuben Kinkaid called a *"ten year old who had the brains of a forty year old midget."*

Christopher and little Tracy with her doll and sweet face were still small fry, of course, but the older kids were quite capable of taking care of them. Barring the unexpected—

Shirley Partridge pushed disturbing images from her mind and walked to the coffee table where the letter-size yellow community newspaper still lay where Laurie had tossed it. *The Meadowville Gazette.* Four pages of local news and gossip. Shirley plopped down on the long lounge with its pattern of sunflowers and picked it up again. The engagement at the Twilight Room was still a week away and the kids did need brushing up on their guitars, drums, tambourines and singing, but it had seemed a fine idea to let them go off and be children again on their own terms. Shirley didn't want them to become Show Biz freaks with no childhood to speak of—no matter how wonderful it was for them to be talented and sophisticated and to number people like Johnny Cash, Tom Jones and Englebert Humperdinck among their acquaintances! Why, they were even on a first-name basis with Ed Sullivan! No, sir, Shirley was no Show Business mother who drove the kids to impossible heights simply in order to make a

14

lot of money. For one thing, she was part of the act herself. For another, she was still a vibrant, lovely woman. Even with five growing children bringing up her rear. Like five cars tacked onto a locomotive.

As she scanned the front page of the newspaper with its blaring advertisement of the Fair, the pale lights of the living room revealed a soft, peaches-and-cream face still remarkably young and a trimly elegant figure whose covering garb of slacks, shirtwaist and sandals might have been envied by any teenager half her age.

Quite realistically, though the children never saw her in that way, of course, she was an eminently attractive, highly appealing woman. A solid fact which Reuben Kinkaid thoroughly applauded, all the while wondering how she could remain unmarried for so long, even with the encumbrance of five little Partridges.

Shirley Partridge, her concern mounting, looked long and hard at the front page of *The Meadowville Gazette*.

In the frame of mind she was in, the announcements of times and events were an almost irritating reminder of how long the kids had been at the Fair. Too long, no matter how you looked at it.

Nostalgia stirred within her, however, as the black type on marigold paper struck her eyes:

Meadowville Picnic Games:

Candy Kisses Hunt
Girls under 5
Boys under 5
Penny Hunt
Girls 5 and 6
Boys 5 and 6
1 Legged Race
Girls 7 and 8
3 Legged Race
Boys 7 and 8

(Christopher and Tracy could run like deer . . .)

Cup and Saucer
Girls 9 and 10

15

Shoe Search Race
Girls 11 and 12
Balloon Breaking
Boys 9 and 10

(Danny ought to score in that competition!)

Egg Throwing
Boys 13 and 14

Shirley Partridge laid the paper down with a barely audible sigh.

There didn't seem to be anything for Keith and Laurie at the Fair except the pleasure of being Big Brother and Big Sister while the siblings had a ball. Still, it ought to be fun, anyway. Plenty of fresh air—the sun had been blazing all day— hot dogs, ice cream, corn on the cob, popcorn, the works. Shirley had given them a twenty dollar bill to play around with.

But, as Life so often shows us, Ignorance is bliss.

Keith Partridge and Laurie Partridge had found quite a lot to do at the Meadowville County Fair. Without throwing an egg, breaking a balloon, searching for a penny or running one-legged or three-legged, the Partridge teenagers had found a new way of life. All on a golden summer afternoon.

And thereby hangs the tale.

So Shirley Partridge fretted and fumed, alternately watching the clock and studying ten closely printed pages of the Twilight Room contract while her offspring cavorted no more than seven miles away in Regan Park where the Fair was in full progress.

She had no way of knowing that what Keith and Laurie had found on the green grass of Regan Park that day was to affect the whole family—and indeed put the entire future of the Partridge Family as a singing group in jeopardy.

Double jeopardy.

In the persons of Keith and Laurie Partridge.

And Reuben Kinkaid would have to gnash his teeth, pull his thatch of blond hair, and maneuver like a Machiavelli to solve the perplexing problems. The centuries-old enigma of *what do you do with a growing child? Growing children?*

Mother Nature, of course, says let them grow.

But it isn't as simple as all that.

Along the route, there are many hardships, heartaches and pains. Agonies and ecstasies, but pains all the same.

16

They call them *growing* pains.

And nobody who has ever been blessed with life has ever found a way to avoid them.

On the last page of *The Meadowville Gazette*, if Shirley Partridge had wanted to look for it, was a small printed announcement. No more than two lines, it was worth knowing, however:

In the event of rain, all festivities will be held the following day, July 31st. General Chairman Leo Rampkin will decide the postponement.

It did not rain, however.

Though it ought to have as far as Shirley Partridge was concerned. Buckets of Jupiter Pluvius might have fixed everything.

General Chairman Leo Rampkin was to prove a catalyst in *L'Affaire* Partridge Family. A humdinger of a catalyst.

Or more appropriately, one of the main straws that broke the camel's back.

In two very important places.

2

HAPPINESS IS A HOT DOG AND GOD KNOWS WHAT ELSE

☐ Danny Partridge, thatch of red hair almost crimson in the bright sunlight, munched contentedly on a hot dog. Tracy Partridge, heedless of his pleasure, was busily devouring a white cloud of cotton candy that almost concealed her pretty little face. Christopher Partridge was too intent on a juicy, buttery ear of corn on the cob to pay much attention to his brother or sister, either. As you see, the Partridges were individuals all.

The Meadowville Fair grounds, a wide-open plateau of tents, stands and game pitches of all descriptions, was a tumult of noise and activity. Mothers and fathers and little children of all sizes and ages overran the spacious area allotted for Meadowville's annual picnic. A helicopter, which could be hired for a three-dollar ride over the scene, was merrily buzzing in the blue sky like some automated insect from a far-off future of science fiction. There was a festive aura of fun and games in the air. And the hours had swept on in a mad whirl of participation and pleasure.

As Shirley Partridge had suspected, Christopher and Tracy had acquitted themselves well in the Leg Races. In fact, Tracy had come in first in her class, winning another doll in the process. Christopher had come in second in his field and for awhile he had inwardly fumed at his little sister's victory.

As for Danny, he had had a miserable time in the balloon breaking event. He hadn't broken enough balloons because his financial turn of mind had been too wrapped up in exactly what amount the Fair would show for a profit that day. Still and all, as it always is with children, last things began to recede in memory and for the full and glorious present, the three smallest Partridges were all involved with their hot dog, cotton candy and corn on the cob, respectively. The twenty-dollar bill which Shirley had given to Keith, as the oldest child, had already been heavily bitten into.

Danny wiped some mustard from his thumb and squinted around at the ambling crowds. His bright eyes counted noses.

"Hey," he said suddenly but without too much concern, "where's Keith and Laurie?"

"They went that way," Tracy mumbled from behind her mound of cotton candy, poking a forefinger toward the wide-open greensward which lay far beyond the stalls of livestock and animal exhibits.

"What for?" Danny grunted.

Christopher raised his face from the half-eaten ear of corn.

"Ball game. Or something. Want to go watch?"

Danny shrugged. "Okay. Wonder why Laurie went. Girls' softball or something?"

"Nah," Tracy said. "Ladies don't play baseball."

"I said softball," Danny snorted. "You dum-dum, there's a difference."

"All right. If you say so," Tracy agreed, amiably enough.

Christopher chomped noisily into his corn.

"It's a boy's game. Didn't you see it on the program? For teenagers. I kind of think Keith wanted to get in on it."

"Then let's go see," Danny suggested. "We've seen everything else, haven't we? And it's still early. We don't have to go home yet. Besides, I'd like to study the game. There's a lot of money to be made playing ball, too. Just like in the music business."

With that, he brushed off his hands and dropped the tissue which had surrounded his hot dog into a nearby trash basket. Tracy straggled along behind him, indifferent to everything but her cotton candy. Still polishing off the corn on the cob, Christopher brought up the rear. Danny threaded his way through the crowds. Beyond the tents and the sounds of revelry, he could just barely make out the unmistakable sound of a bat making contact with a ball. And the roar of noise so

20

particular to a crowd that watches diamond play of some kind. For Danny who had played street ball and all sorts of boys' sports, there was no specific inducement in the sound, though. He was far too busy being a miniature financial giant to have the normal amount of interest that a ten-year-old boy should have in sports.

Not so Keith Partridge.

For so very suddenly that it came like a blast of magic, Keith had rediscovered his childhood somewhere between four and six o'clock that sunny afternoon.

And standing on the sidelines, rooting him on, Laurie Partridge had found something else. Something named Leo Rampkin who had blue blue eyes, white white teeth and broad broad shoulders and black black hair. All of it curled, wavy and unforgettably groovy.

Leo Rampkin and Softball were the two major reasons why the Partridge Family were so long at the Fair that afternoon.

Keith Partridge had gone in to play right field. At seventeen, he was still growing and his limber body was lean and athletic with as yet not fully developed muscles. Laurie had urged him to get into the game because when she caught sight of Leo Rampkin getting the game lined up, choosing sides and generally running things, his impact had hit her right between the eyes. He had smiled at her warmly when Keith stepped forward. Leo was a college teacher of outstanding merits and qualifications at the ripe old age of twenty-two, and Meadowville and its merchant sponsors had readily turned over its Fair to the Gifted Young, trying hard like everybody else to span the Generation Gap. It was a friendly and shrewd gesture to which all of Meadowville's younger people had responded. The Fair was going along swimmingly. A sure-fire hit all down the line and now this ballgame was the final stroke of psychological acumen. Meadowville's young men, sideburned, moustached and long-haired though they were, were now engaged in playing baseball. Rather than involving themselves in protests, riots and student demonstrations. It was a good thing, all around.

Keith had taken up his position on the greensward, half in the spirit of a lark and being a good sport. But in no time at all, something in him had responded to a long dormant urge.

It was as if he had just discovered the magic of competition.

21

Laurie placed herself advantageously close to tall Leo Rampkin along the first base line. There were no seats available and everybody had to stand in knots of people to form the crowd, but nobody seemed to mind. Least of all, Laurie. Leo brushed up against her as the excitement of the game bore onward. And out in right field, Keith Partridge, a young boy who earned his living as a professional musician, suddenly became the reincarnation of Ty Cobb, Joe DiMaggio, Mel Ott and Ted Williams. And the crowd roared, caught up in the full fever of a grand ballgame on a glorious summer afternoon.

A batter at the plate caught hold of an outside pitch and drove it a country mile toward right field. Keith, fluidly and with great skill and grace, drifted far back to his left, ranging like a gazelle and brought the ball down without a wasted motion. The crowd thundered its acclaim. And before the inning was done, he had reversed the process, zooming in at top speed across the grass to make a diving, sitting-down catch of a Texas League pop fly that threatened to fall in for a damaging hit with two men on base. He trotted in from his position, the third out still tucked in his glove, and Meadowville gave him what had to amount to a standing ovation. Keith's grin was wide with appreciation and his blood tingled at the response. A thousand times more than it ever had at a Las Vegas opening, for instance, when the fans had applauded the Partridge Family for their musical showmanship.

Leo Rampkin applauded warmly and looked down at Laurie, whose lovely face hung poised at his shoulder.

"That's pretty professional outfielding," he marveled aloud. "Your brother ever play ball anywhere before?"

Laurie shook her head. "He's a musician. And a good one. You ought to hear him on guitar."

"I have all the Partridge Family record albums," Leo said, laughing, but his eyes were curiously alert. "But he must have played ball somewhere before. Either that or he's a natural—"

"Then he's a natural," Laurie sighed. She couldn't have cared less. "Have your eyes always been blue, Leo?"

He stared down at her and she suddenly blushed deep red, realizing the stupid thing she had said, all unthinkingly.

"No," he said, responding in kind. "One was orange and the other green before I was six years old. A terrible lightning storm shocked them both into the same color."

Laurie lowered her gaze to hide the blush, but Leo Rampkin laughed not unkindly, and the awkward moment was over.

Danny, Tracy and Christopher joined the game just as Keith came up to the plate. There was a man on first and third as the result of two soft singles, but a pair of outs sandwiched in between had put Keith's team in a position to score. The pitcher for the other side was a wicked underhander with a blazing fast ball and the kids looked on in awe as he poured two fast strikes over the plate. Keith had never taken the bat off his shoulder. But Leo Rampkin, oblivious of Laurie's admiration, was watching him very carefully. Keith hadn't been fooled—he had taken the pitches, looking them over with all the aplomb of say a Ted Williams. The pitcher unwisely underrated him, coming back with another fast ball instead of wasting one the way any sensible pitcher might have.

Even those in the crowd who were not too familiar with the strange mores of a ball game were not oblivious to what happened next. The runners broke from first and third as the pitcher released the ball. It zipped toward home plate on a blurred line. Keith Partridge shifted on his heels smoothly, the bat cocked and rotated with dizzying speed and then came that sound like no other in the entire spectrum of the sports world: *CRACK!*

Every eye in that packed meadow strained to follow the flight of a ball which suddenly rocketed over the infield, gained the heights of majesty and then literally soared out of view. There was no outfield fence for it to clear but there was a bedazzled outfielder who turned, tried to catch up with a bird in flight and couldn't, and watched helplessly as the ball came down in the heart of the small oval lake a good fifty feet behind the playing field. Keith Partridge trotted around the bases, with a three-run homer to his credit, and the adulation of the crowd reached a frenzy.

It was a home run worthy of an embryonic Babe Ruth and the sort of swat he must have registered when he too was only a stripling boy ready to bewilder and amuse the baseball universe.

"Did Keith hit the ball?" little Tracy murmured, seeing all the activity on the bases and not quite understanding it.

"Hit it?" Danny echoed. "He pulverized it!"

"Gee, I wish I had another corn on the cob," Christopher

23

muttered, who had stooped to retrieve a bag of marbles he had won for finishing second in his leg race. "That was good."

Laurie clapped her hands delightedly, happy that Brother Keith was making such a fine impression on Leo Rampkin. Leo had moved up to personally congratulate Keith on the wonderful hit that put his team three runs ahead. Keith accepted the plaudits in a daze, not too sure of the strange and wonderful fever flooding his insides. His blood was singing; never had he felt so heady or important. Or admired.

The remainder of the game did nothing to reduce the overpowering sense of a new-found wonder and elation. If anything, it was thrill piled upon thrill. Deed stacked upon accomplishment and one of those kinds of days that every ballplayer on this earth should have. And certainly every boy born of woman.

Playing a guitar with a family singing act just couldn't hold a candle to this. How could it? It was something he was doing alone, collaborating with no one else—he was manufacturing all the thrills and excitement and wonder all by his lonesome.

Did he ever!

In the third inning, he came up again with a man on second and promptly sent a long double between the center and left fielders that easily scored another run. He scored himself when the next man shot a single past the infield and beat the relay from the outfield home with a neat, hooking slide around the catcher. When he got up, dusting off his pants, the crowd went wild. The score was 5-0 now and he had knocked in four of the runs and scored the fifth himself.

In the next inning, with the other fellows threatening—they had loaded the bases after two were out—once again the boy in right field responded to the occasion. With a headlong, over-the-shoulder catch of a wicked line drive heading for the outfield grass.

The game wore on in a frenzy of base hits and spectacular plays.

Keith came up in the sixth inning and though he only singled, it was as if he had hit another home run. The din was terrific.

And then came the historic last inning. The inning that was to become the talk of Meadowville for many long winters to come. By this time, hundreds more people had drifted over from the Fair grounds proper, brought to the scene by vocal reports of the exciting game in progress.

In the top of the inning, behind five runs, the opposition rallied as the easily winning pitcher suddenly folded in the heat. The leadoff man tripled, the next batter doubled, there followed a set of three singles. And then before order could be restored, a big hefty boy named Moose Towner plastered a pitch far beyond the left field grass for a long homer and suddenly, Keith's team was behind 7-5. Keith saved the inning from becoming a complete shambles with an electrifyingly accurate throw from the outfield that cut down the eighth run of the inning trying to score from second on a single to right field. The crowd ate up that play too and when he came running in, the fever in his brain and heart had reached a crescendo of discovery and excitement. Was playing ball always as soul-satisfying as this? Nothing he had ever done on a guitar had ever made him feel like this! So *heady*, so excited . . .

And there was more to come.

Down to the last out, Keith's team rallied in the do-or-die seventh. Paul Walters singled and Johnny Leslie doubled, and once again Keith came up with two men on base. Second and third, this time.

Leo Rampkin shook his head. Laurie saw the gesture and frowned.

"Something wrong?"

"Nothing."

"But you look funny—come on. What is it?"

Keith braced himself in the batter's box and the crowd was roaring again. The runners danced off the base paths.

"The law of averages," Leo Rampkin said, bitterly. "Bound to catch up with him, I'd say."

"I still don't know what you mean."

"Laurie," Leo said patiently, "your brother, God bless him, has homered with two men on, doubled with a man on, singled on his third trip, already knocked in four runs of the five they've got and scored the other one, made three of the best catches I've ever seen in my life and slid home like Ty Cobb and threw a runner out at the plate like Willie Mays in his prime—he can't be expected to do it again. He just can't. So don't be disappointed if he doesn't deliver this time."

25

"Oh, I don't know," Laurie said, airily. "You don't know my brother Keith."

"And you just don't know baseball. Even Ted Williams only made three and a half hits every ten times he came to bat and he was only the best hitter that ever lived."

"You just wait and see."

On the sidelines, oblivious of all this, Danny, Christopher and even little Tracy were adding their vocal support to Keith at the plate with whistles and yells and stamping of feet. Keith was like Gibraltar in the batter's box. Calm, steady, his eyes on no one but the man on the mound, holding onto the big white ball.

The crowd did not let up and when the first *"Strike!"* was called it was like the legendary Casey at the Bat. Noise sailed down from the crowds. Riotous, overwhelming noise. But the pitcher, aware of the identity of the batter, and just as cool as ever, fired the ball back. Keith swung and fouled it off. *"Strike Two!"* the man umpiring behind home plate bellowed.

Now only that ephemeral third strike stood between Keith, the pitcher and a humiliating 7-5 loss. More so because Keith's team had led 5-0 going into the fatal seventh.

Again the pitcher set up and fired the ball in. The crowd held its breath. Again, Keith fouled it off. The count held. Two strikes, no balls. Laurie felt her own heart stop beating, Danny set his mouth in a grim line. Leo Rampkin looked on, quietly and shrewdly, wondering if the Law of Averages could be set aside just this once. He sincerely hoped so.

The pitcher rocked once more, whipped his arm under and down and the ball sped toward the plate. The crowd barely *aahed* as Keith swung his bat. And then the *aah* transformed into a wildly exultant, ear-shattering din of disbelief, gladness and sheer awe. For the heroics of a local celebrity named Keith Partridge who all of a sudden seemed to be a heller with a bat. Mickey Mantle at the very least!

CRACK!

For the second time that amazing afternoon, the white ball soared out of sight, rocketing in orbit until it dropped like a golf tee shot into the little oval lake far beyond the playing field. Long before Keith Partridge could circle the bases, his face split into the biggest smile since the first Christmas, the crowds had surged onto the playing field, swept him to their shoulders and borne him aloft in a mad, riotous parade of tri-

26

umph. For the first time in Meadowville history, an average ball game had been turned into a festival of joy and wonder. It had not been *just another ball game.*

Danny Partridge stood up proudly and surveyed the scene, his arms folded, his smile a victorious smirk.

"The Partridge Family," he announced loudly. "A hit, as usual."

No one heard him. Everybody was too busy yelling and shouting and heaping hosannahs on the senior slugger of the game.

"Well," Laurie Partridge said to Leo Rampkin as they fought their way through the crowd to Keith Partridge, "so much for your Law of Averages. Guess Keith showed you, didn't he?"

"Uh huh," Leo Rampkin agreed, glad to be a good loser. "Guitar player, is he? I think we'll see about that."

In such innocuous-sounding remarks is the course of history affected. Changed, transformed, redirected, rechanneled.

In this case, Partridge Family history.

Leo Rampkin, all unwittingly, was about to rock their boat very very dangerously.

Something for which he would not be thanked, little loved and generally hated by one Reuben Kinkaid.

Keith Partridge's field day with the bat and the glove and the singing in his youthful veins had written a new page in the nearly always exciting life of the Partridge Family.

Mighty Partridge, unlike the hapless Casey of old, had *not* struck out. It might have been better for all concerned if he had.

As it was, Keith was in a transport of glory.

He felt as if he could do just about anything in the whole wide world. And a guitar suddenly seemed like a very childish, very foolish instrument. Compared to a baseball bat, that is.

And Laurie Partridge, eyes glowing proudly and happily, clung to the side of groovy Leo Rampkin. Her alive feminine mind was already spinning some day dreams of its own.

Why, the long hot day at the Meadowville Fair had just about turned out to be the greatest day in her life, too!

She was justly convinced, unshakably so, that she had finally met Mr. Right.

Leo Rampkin.

Blue-eyed, broad-shouldered, curly-headed yet and just plain magnificent!

What an entry she would have for her leather-bound pink diary that very night—

Leo Rampkin was ever so *relevant*—which was just about Laurie Partridge's favorite, operative word.

3

REUBEN, REUBEN

☐ Reuben Kinkaid, the successful manager of the very successful Partridge Family, was having a container of coffee in his modern office on the third floor of the Hendricks Building. Reuben was in a very good mood.

He was freshly shaved, smartly dressed, hummingly happy. And with very good reason. His secretary Arlene had just placed in the mail another bountiful recording contract from Emko Recording Company. The contract was for four figures and all it stipulated was that Emko wanted to hire the Partridges for one more studio session wherein the group would wax their very popular club act—the one which had been such a smash all over the country. Details had been worked out and all that was needed was the signature of Shirley Partridge to cement the deal. All in all, on top of the very lucrative and forthcoming Twilight Room engagement, the Partridges were rapidly about to augment their income for the year very handsomely.

Reuben was always a very busy man. He usually ate his meals on the fly, between trains, in airplane seats and once in a very great while, he did find the time during office hours to send down to the luncheonette in the lobby for a coffee and Danish. Reuben had no ulcers—yet—but he was treading the rocky road of managerial tactics which so often leads to one.

Arlene came in as he was sipping his coffee and wrinkled her nose at him. She was a very attractive blonde but not quite as bright as Reuben would have liked her to be. However, he was a fair man always and was giving her typing and office brain a lot of time in which to develop.

"You wanted those contracts to go Registered, didn't you, Mr. Kinkaid?"

"But def, Arlene." He put down his empty container and smiled at her. "With the proper amount of postage, too, I hope."

"I thought so." She sighed. "Well, that's how it went."

"Now," Reuben sighed. "You see? There's hope for you yet, my girl."

She almost blushed. "Thanks, Mr. Kinkaid."

"Think nothing of it."

She still stood, hesitant, on the threshold. Reuben, still in a fine mood, especially since she had not snarled up the mailing instructions, smiled up at her magnanimously.

"Was there anything else, Arlene?"

"Huh?" She looked blank.

He rocked forward in his chair and adjusted his tie.

"You look like you're trying to remember something—" he began.

"Oh!" Suddenly, she snapped her fingers and her eyes grew round and big. "Phone call for you. One three three. Somebody named Borden. Or Gordon—I think—"

Reuben did not lose his temper. He smiled sweetly and reached for the phone. He hummed gently under his breath. He always did when he felt like swearing.

"How long ago?" he asked very quietly.

"Just a minute. I was coming in to tell you when I remembered about the mail."

"Why didn't you use the Inter-Com? That's what it was invented for, my girl."

"Oh." She snapped her fingers again. "Now why didn't I think of that? I will next time, Mr. Kinkaid. I promise."

"Thanks, muchly. Now if you'll go back to your desk, I'll take the call, Arlene."

"Sure, Mr. Kinkaid."

With the door closed, he shut his eyes and heaved a mammoth shrug. Then he opened them again, punched the button on his phone set and leaned back in his chair.

"Kinkaid here, Gordon."

Despite Arlene's willy-nilly memory, it had to be no one but Barney Gordon, the peppery byliner of one of the biggest newspaper columns on the circuit. *By Ear* by Barney Gordon was a barometer of everything that happened in the music and recording business.

"Reuben, I need a beat."

"I haven't got one. Except that the Partridges are climbing on all the charts, and you know about Emko Recording and the Twilight Room."

"Reuben, isn't there a whisper of romance in Shirley Partridge's life? Doesn't anybody make her heart beat faster? Think of the scoop it would give me."

"It would give me heart failure," Reuben chuckled. "Sorry, Barney. Shirley's devoted to the kids. No time for herself, no time for romance. All the news that's fit to print about the Partridges will never make the front pages of anything but *Variety*. And that's the way I want it. Don't ask for waves where there aren't any."

Barney Gordon snorted from his end of the line.

"Young beautiful woman like that—it's a shame."

"Sure it is."

"If she ever does find someone she likes, I'll be the first to know, Reuben?"

"You'll be the first to know, Barney."

"Scout's honor?"

"Scout's honor."

After Barney Gordon had rung off, Reuben Kinkaid settled back in his comfortable chair with a luxurious murmur of contentment. All things being equal, he was very glad Shirley Partridge was the sort of woman she was. A romance in her life would only spoil the normal even keel of a ship that was going places. Let love come last—it was harsh, perhaps, but that's Show Biz!

Being a manager was difficult enough without personal problems shaking the *status quo*.

His role as business manager to the Partridges was deeper than that, of course, but it did make his job a lot easier when all the family paid their full devotion and attention to their jobs.

The jobs of being singers and entertainers.

Sun streamed onto Reuben Kinkaid's desk from the windows behind him. He basked in the golden beams and envisioned piles of Midas matter building higher and higher as the Partridge Family rose to the top of their chosen field.

Poor man.

How was he to know that the pot was brewing in Meadow-ville and events and motivations were stirring that even in his most clairvoyant moments he could not have foreseen.

Baseball and Love had come to the Partridge Family.

If not in equal doses, certainly potent ones.

They had missed the last bus home from the Fair. But there was no problem, really. As far as Laurie Partridge was concerned, it was a gift from heaven. Handsome Leo Rampkin had readily offered to drive the Partridges home in his station wagon. A large beaten-up machine with a good motor and plenty of room. But Laurie managed to park herself on the front seat with Leo while Keith and Danny and Tracy and Christopher piled up in the rear. The kids were in an ecstatic frame of mind, thanks to Keith's ballplaying heroics. As for Keith, he was still experiencing that inner awe of *discovery*. To learn that he could do something else besides play a guitar and do that thing exceptionally well, was mind-boggling. The cheers and plaudits of the enthusiastic crowd had truly gone to his head. He was in an euphoria of temperament and happiness.

In fact, it was difficult for him to speak.

His mind was filled with visions of playing in a nice white uniform before an enormously packed stadium somewhere in the major leagues and hitting one game-winning homer after the other.

And his dreams were getting better all the while.

Up front, Leo Rampkin steered the station wagon briskly through the last-second traffic emptying out from the Fair, took the winding dirt road toward the highway and put his thoughts together. He *did* have an ulterior motive for taking the Partridges home. What Keith had shown him on the ball field indicated a gift of no little matter. The question was— what to do with it?

After all, Keith Partridge already had a career. And one that loomed fabulously. A major cog and part of a hit singing family group. What would he want with a baseball career?

He winked at Keith in the rear-view mirror and the young man smiled back. Keith's face was still dusty and stained from the game.

"Laurie tells me you never played much ball before, Keith," Leo offered for openers.

"Uh uh," Keith said, tiredly. "Too much school work, helping Mom with the kids."

"You're pretty good, you know."

"I got lucky."

Leo shook his head. "Four for four is never lucky. Not when two of those hits are homers at the right time. And your fielding. Like Joe DiMaggio in his prime."

"Joe DiMaggio?" Tracy piped up. "What a funny name. Who's that?"

Keith squinted. "Yeah. I read about him a few times. He was good, huh?"

"The best," Leo said firmly. "He was before my time but my Dad talked about him all the time. And I am kind of interested in baseball so I'm up on the *Little Red Book*. DiMaggio is considered by many the greatest ballplayer of his day."

"Huh," Danny Partridge sniffed. "Bet he can't play the guitar like Keith can."

"No, he couldn't," Leo admitted, with a laugh. "But he was good enough to earn one hundred thousand dollars a season as a centerfielder for the New York Yankees."

Now, Danny was impressed. "No fooling, Mr. Rampkin?"

"No fooling." Almost casually, Leo then said softly, "Ever think about playing baseball for a living, Keith?"

Keith shook his head.

"You could, you know. Very easily. At your age you could get a tryout with some major league outfit and then be sent to one of their farm clubs and before you know it—"

Laurie Partridge snorted.

"My brother Keith? He's not tall enough. Or heavy enough."

"He's a growing boy," Leo said very patiently. "That's what farm clubs are for. To develop a boy while he's growing to his adult height and weight."

Keith, as interested as he was, shook his head almost sheepishly. "Heck, I couldn't do that. Break up the act? What would Mom and the kids do without me playing lead guitar?"

But inside his alive young mind, the thought had already taken hold, finding ready handholds on his dreams of big crowds, game-winning hits and all that acclaim thundering down from the stands. Gee—what a thrill it was!

Leo persisted, somewhat strangely, Laurie thought.

"Mind if I discuss it with your mother, Keith?"

"Sure. Mom'll talk to anybody about anything but it's a way-out idea, Mr. Rampkin. Honest it is."

"Fair enough." Leo Rampkin increased the speed of the station wagon on the smooth highway. A flow of late evening traffic was in motion, steadily going North.

Laurie changed the subject.

"How would you like to stay for supper, Mr. Rampkin?"

"What's this Mr. Rampkin all of a sudden? You were calling me Leo at the ball game—"

Laurie smiled. "I was being formal because I was inviting you to dinner. Say for being nice enough to take us home."

"Hadn't you better wait until you see how your mother cottons to the idea? After all, she's the one who has to cook."

"Mom will like the idea," Laurie said, positively. "She approves of men who are schoolteachers. And good ones, at that."

"Thank you, milady. How does the idea sit with the rest of you?"

"Glad to have you," Danny said authoritatively.

"Sure," Keith agreed. "I want to talk to you some more about Joe DiMaggio."

Tracy laughed again. "What a cute name that is! Isn't it a cute name, Christopher?"

Christopher shrugged.

"It's all right, I guess. But it's not nearly as nice a name as Engelbert Humperdinck."

Everybody laughed at that, and soon Leo Rampkin was turning off the highway into the side street that led toward the Partridge home where it nestled on a nice quiet block surrounded with the centuries-old shade of sturdy willows, elms and ash trees.

The sun had gone down behind the low range of buildings from downtown proper. The landscape was flooded with the soft filtering rays of a brilliant sunlight. The green of the trees was almost poetic in the seven o'clock daylight.

Not unsurprisingly, Shirley Partridge was standing on the wide veranda that fronted the house. Even as Leo Rampkin wheeled into the driveway, he could see the worried expression on her face transform into a fleeting flicker of annoyance.

Mother Partridge was glad to see her chicks safely home at last.

But also, she didn't look very happy about the lateness of the hour. Somebody should have had the good sense to at least telephone about being delayed.

Which, of course, nobody had.

But there was more than the clock involved, as Shirley was soon to learn.

The love bug and the baseball bug had struck that afternoon at Meadowville County Fair.

Each in its own inexplicable, unforeseen way.

Reuben Kinkaid's plans for the Twilight Room and the Emko Recording Company were to receive a very severe setback.

The growing pains of the Partridge children were entering into the scheme of things.

And before the week was out, something less than heaven was going to break out!

4

THE COLD SHOULDER

☐ Leo Rampkin was indeed invited for dinner.

Shirley Partridge was extremely pleased with him for being kind enough to drive the kids home. But somewhere between appetizers and dessert (which was chocolate pudding with whipped cream, something Tracy and Christopher absolutely adored) she began to regret her decision. She was over her slight pique with the kids for being late and not having the common sense to make a phone call saying as much and she could see that Leo was the sort of young man all males should be like. He was handsome, clean-cut, alert and on the side of the angels, obviously, but something inside her female soul grew frightened as the details of the afternoon slowly came forth during mealtime. She learned all about Tracy's winning the foot race and Danny's Second Best at balloon-breaking but the account of Keith's ball game was positively fantastic.

Her uneasiness stemmed from a very simple source.

Her son, Keith Partridge.

As Leo Rampkin recited the heroics of the game with Keith's name all too prominent in the account, she couldn't take her eyes off her son's face. Never had she seen him so happy. So *alive* to something. So enthusiastic. Not even solos on his guitar before packed clubs had elicited so much joy and wonder. Nor did Leo's repeated suggestions and indications that Keith had all the potential for a ballplayer's career set her mind at ease. It did her heart good to see Keith so happy, so much like the teenage boy he was, but somewhere inside her brain, vague storm warnings were beginning to sound. And one look at Laurie's shining face (she couldn't take *her* eyes off Leo Rampkin) and she also knew that her eldest daughter was now experiencing one of her very strongest crushes.

Still, it was all something that *could* pass.

The excitement of this day could wear off. Or could it?

"Pass the butter," Danny snapped at Tracy, who was closest to the dish.

"*Please*," Shirley reminded him sternly, smiling at Leo Rampkin. "*Please*," growled Danny, and Tracy passed the butter dish. Leo studied Shirley Partridge and liked what he saw. She was a very attractive woman, younger looking than he had expected.

"You know, Mrs. Partridge," he continued, "the way Keith plays he just might be something special. And there's no reason why he couldn't have two careers. Baseball is only part of the year—"

Danny nodded, vigorously.

"Unless you don't know, Mom, Mr. Rampkin says some players earn as much as one hundred thousand dollars a year. Gee. Even Mister Kinkaid can't guarantee me a salary like that."

"Joe, Joe DiMaggio . . ." Tracy sang. "I like that name. He's a hunderd thousand dollar ballplayer, Mom."

Laurie Partridge, eager to impress Leo Rampkin, put her two cents in.

"Can you imagine what a gate attraction Keith would be if he starred for say the Mets and played music with us too?"

Shirley Partridge folded her hands and smiled at all of them, hiding that inner feeling of uneasiness she couldn't quite have explained to anyone, least of all herself.

"One ball game," she said slowly, "does not a ballplayer make. DiMaggio and all those people who are and were so good at baseball put in years of apprenticeship before they made good. I'm sure Mr. Rampkin knows that as well as I do."

"Call me Leo, please," Rampkin said. "It's silly for you to call me Mister."

"Sure," Christopher piped up. "Let's call him Leo."

"All right, Leo," Shirley said. "Let's put it this way. Keith is a very important member of the Partridge Family. He plays guitar. Playing one ball game at a Fair is fun. But if he did it for a living, he might break a finger or a hand. Or something. And then where would he be? Besides, next week we play a very special engagement at the Twilight Club and—" She stopped talking because she suddenly realized she was running on, defending her position to this comparative stranger. And poor Keith's face had fallen to his shoetops.

Again, the alarm bell rang inside her.

She forced herself to stop talking and looked at Keith.

"Well, Slugger. How about it? You want to say something? After all it's your future we're discussing. Mr. Rampkin, Leo, seems to think you have what it takes to be a major leaguer. What do you think?"

Keith looked sheepish, his eyes traveling around the table and resting on Leo Rampkin's approving smile.

"Gosh, Mom. I agree with you. One game doesn't make me any star. But gee whiz—I can't explain what it was like out there. Being able to hit the ball like that, making those catches. Coming through in the clutch." He shook his head and lowered his eyes. "Sure felt good. Something special. Something *else* . . . I just never felt that way before. Not ever."

"I see," Shirley Partridge said quietly. "And I do understand. I remember when I danced the part of The Good Fairy in my high school play. I thought I was going to be the greatest ballerina since Pavlova but then I graduated and met your father and—" She paused, shaking off a very happy yet very sad memory. "Well, you have all the time in the world to think about it. After this season is over, if you think you'd like to try it—"

Keith's face came up, red.

"Mom! I'd never run out on you and the family. You need me. Don't you?"

This last remark was so tentative and halting, Shirley's heart went right out to him.

"Don't know what I'd do without you, Keith Partridge and that's a fact. So there. Put that in your pipe and smoke it."

Leo Rampkin had not graduated college with highest honors for nothing. He discreetly dropped the subject and the table talk went on to more mundane things. Shirley discussed the success of the Fair with him, the local rock festival which had caused so much fun and talk the month before, and other matters that involved the teenage problems of the day. As a dynamic and successful teacher, Leo had a lot of ideas about the Generation Gap.

But even as she talked with the young man, with Laurie putting her oar in every chance she could, she was all too aware of the light in Keith Partridge's eyes. She knew her own family too well. She could tell when Tracy was fibbing, when Christopher hadn't slept well and when Laurie and Danny were having one of their frequent disagreements about the state of the world. She also knew that her son Keith was still hopelessly smitten with what had obviously happened to him that afternoon. His face was wreathed in a glaze of sheer rapture.

When he excused himself from the table after dinner to go into the den for something or other and he was humming *Take Me Out To The Ball Game,* her worst fears were realized.

Keith had very suddenly discovered the great and grand sport of Baseball, the National Pastime.

For some boys it can be fatal.

A love that can cling to them for the rest of their lives.

A passion that can make everything else in the world come second.

Including family, a musical career and Lord only knew what else!

Still, there was also the small but nettling fact that Keith might be every bit as good as Leo Rampkin seemed to think he was.

And if he was—then what?

Shirley Partridge just didn't know how to answer that question.

It was all up to, when you got right down to hard facts, Keith Partridge. *A To Be Or Not To Be* situation, just like Shakespeare's *Hamlet.* And everybody knew how that poor Dane had turned out. A wreck, just because he couldn't make up his mind.

After dinner, Shirley invited Leo Rampkin into the living room where everybody sat around listening to record albums and generally having a fine time. But even as the room rocked with good music, Shirley couldn't take her mind off

40

the dim ogre which had suddenly reared its unlovely head in her household.

What was worse, she couldn't even give the orgre a proper name.

All she did know was that it was there all the same, vague and ghostlike, and threatening the safety and security of the Partridge nest. Things were going so well and to have this faint, troublesome, unknown thing in the house was disturbing.

Laurie danced with Leo and Danny and Tracy and Christopher clapped hands, setting up a tempo before they broke out their instruments and rendered some impromptu band work. Jumpy music that throbbed.

Keith Partridge didn't come down from the den until much later.

When he did, Shirley was quick to note that he was jauntily wearing his old baseball cap, the one he had worn in high school, and his grin was as big and wide as the Missouri River.

Now, she was convinced.

Keith was flaunting his sudden new love.

Almost boldly.

The cap made everybody laugh when he loomed into view. And maybe that was the whole idea.

And maybe it wasn't.

About ten-thirty, Leo Rampkin took his leave. He thanked Shirley Partridge for a fine dinner and time, shook hands with all the Partridges. Only Laurie insisted on seeing him out to his car. For Keith, Leo had one parting shot.

"See you around, Ballplayer. And if you have the time and the inclination, come on out to the field Monday night. There's a game you might like to see. Meadowville Diamond. Six o'clock."

Keith's interest made his eyes jump out like electric lights. He stepped in very close to Leo Rampkin.

"Uh—sure. Who's playing?"

"Nothing special. Just a pick-up game. Some of the boys like to keep their hand in. You could take a few swings, have some fun. Okay?"

"You," Keith Partridge said, "got a deal."

Shirley Partridge, very tactfully, said nothing.

With that, Leo Rampkin smiled his goodnight and Laurie

41

accompanied him out to the car. The kids all noisily made their farewells.

It was a beautiful night. The willows, elms and ashes wavered in an evening breeze. A big, almost full moon hung suspended in the sky. Laurie sighed romantically and Leo took her arm as they strolled to the stationwagon, showing clearly in the driveway. A cricket made noises in the bushes. An owl hooted back.

"Well, you certainly made a fine impression on my brother, Leo."

"He made a fine impression on me, Laurie. In fact, your whole family did. I'm about ready to become a real genuine Partridge Family fan. I always liked your music but to find out you're a good bunch of people is something else again."

Laurie sighed again.

"We like you too, Leo. You're a very *relevant* man."

He chuckled. "Thank you. I've been called a lot of things but never that before."

They reached the car and Leo put his hand on the door.

Laurie looked up at him. The moonlight bathed her face in a halo of gentle, soft beauty.

"Leo, tell me something?"

"Sure, Laurie."

"Is Keith really all that good? As good as you seem to think he is?"

Leo Rampkin paused and measured his words very very carefully.

"Let me put it this way. Today could have been a flash in the pan. Just one of those games where everything goes right and you get fooled by what you see. But let me also say this. I coach a lot of ball games. I've played. High school and College. I've seen a lot of big league games. Keith has *natural* ability—you can always tell—he responded automatically this afternoon, made all the moves *without having to think about it*. You understand? He has what they call a born skill. Right now, without going out too far on a limb, I'd dare to say that if he stays with it, he could become a very superior ballplayer. Understand?"

"Wow. That *is* good, huh?"

"It's the very most desired condition for a ballplayer. DiMaggio had it, Mays has it. Mantle, Johnny Bench of the Reds And right now Keith has it. At a very early age, which is the way it should be."

Laurie watched Leo's face, admiring the manner in which his dark, curly hair tumbled over his forehead.

"It was nice of you to tell him. Made him feel fine. I can tell—"

"It was only the truth. Well, good night, Laurie. It was a very pleasant evening. And your mother is a great cook. The pot roast was superb."

"I'll tell her. She liked you, Leo. We all did—and do. We ever going to see you again?"

His grin was masked with the moon behind his broad back.

"If Keith goes to the game Monday, you go with him. Okay?"

"That *is* a date," Laurie said fervently. "I could see he had already made up his mind to go. I think you could lead a horse to water and make him drink even if he didn't want to, Leo Rampkin."

He said no more and started to clamber behind the wheel of the car. Laurie Partridge responded to the mood of the moment. And her own impulsive instincts. She leaned upward and quickly kissed Leo Rampkin's unprepared cheek. Before he could say a word, she whirled on her heels and fled back up the darkened walk toward the house.

Her heart was beating like a triphammer because of her own aggressiveness and daring. Imagine! Kissing a boy on a first date! And it wasn't really and truly and honestly a date!

Somewhat amused but very thoughtful for all of that, Leo Rampkin set the stationwagon in motion, backed slowly out of the driveway and drove quietly off into the night.

At the door of the house, Laurie Partridge watched him go, her heart trembling, her knees like water.

What a wonderful groovy man!

Relevant?

He was just Mr. Right, that's all.

Upstairs in her bedroom, Shirley Partridge slowly undressed. It was after eleven and the kids had all settled down in their rooms. The house was quiet and only an occasional jet plane thundering overhead broke the tranquility of the long summer night.

Shirley had a lot to think about.

And it looked like a restless night for her. She was still vaguely uneasy about the curious events of the day.

Oh, well, she reflected, it all just might pass. Tomorrow

was another day and maybe the excitement and adventure of it all would wear off. But she really didn't think so. And therein lay her uneasiness.

She only regretted that she knew her own children so well. *Too* well, unfortunately. She wasn't their mother for nothing.

Keith, she knew, had discovered a vital new interest. Baseball. Whether it proved good for him or not remained to be seen.

Laurie, she also knew, had discovered a brand new crush. Leo Rampkin. Whether she would outgrow it like all her other passing fancies also remained to be seen.

Time was her strongest ally.

Time which made people outgrow things and move on to other things. Being a mother had its compensations. Experience had taught her that nothing lasts forever. Not even childhood.

But she also knew, all too sadly, that you have to live through it all, just the same. And count not the cost.

Still unsettled and troubled, Shirley Partridge went to bed.

All the Partridges dreamed that night.

Tracy relived the exciting foot race in which she had come in first and won a doll. Beating out her nearest rival, the little blonde girl with braces on her teeth, by as much as ten feet.

Christopher saw himself gorging himself with corn on the cob, wolfing down a whole table full of them His dream was a blaze of maize.

Danny had a pip of a dream.

He envisioned himself smoking a cigar, dressed like a big wheel with fancy clothes and spats, as the manager of Keith Partridge, the star outfielder of the New York Mets who was earning two hundred thousand dollars a year as he batted his team into the World Series. Danny saw himself earning his ten percent, piling one green bill atop the other while Reuben Kinkaid stood in the background, gnashing his teeth, begging Danny to let him have half-interest in Keith's career. The best part of the dream was hearing Mister Kinkaid admit how smart he, Danny, was!

Laurie Partridge had a quieter dream. But no less exciting. She saw herself and Leo Rampkin doing a lot of things together. Dancing, surfing, out driving, playing games together. And best of all was the moment when Leo held her in his arms, kissed her, and asked her to marry him before he went off to join the Peace Corps in Africa. Dear handsome wonderful Leo Rampkin!

As for Keith Partridge, he had the best dream of all.

His mother could not sleep but Keith didn't have that problem. He surrendered to Morpheus as soon as his tired head hit the soft pillow and from that moment on, fantasy, wishful thinking and boyish marvels took complete control of his consciousness.

It was the greatest dream of his life.

Of any boy's life.

5

PARTRIDGE AT THE BAT

☐ It was the ninth inning of the last game of the 1971 World Series between the Baltimore Orioles and the New York Mets. As in all dreams, the stands seemed to bulge with patrons, the lights of the ball park were blinding and a vast sea of noise filled the eardrums. Noise reigned supreme.

Pennants and banners and signs hung all over the park and with the Mets coming to bat in the crucial last inning, the score was 7-4 in favor of the Orioles. Lucky Keith Partridge tensed in his sleep but never had his eyes, his hearing or any of his senses been more acute. The world of his vision encompassed the universe. And sitting along the first base line behind the Mets dugout were Mom and the rest of the kids. Laurie and Danny and Christopher and Tracy. Rooters all, especially for Keith Partridge.

The Orioles and Mets had won three games apiece, and here in the seventh and deciding game, it looked to be all over for New York. Three runs down with but three more outs to their name and the baseball championship of the world at stake. Nobody had any faces for Keith in his dream. Only Mom and the kids. The thousands of fans and the Oriole and Met players were all faceless phantoms, yelling and shouting, darting to and fro at their positions on the field which was as green as a pool table. And a million times larger.

Keith fidgeted in the dugout, anxious and raring to go. To get up there and swing at the ball. His muscles ached for action.

The dream raced on, swiftly and pulsingly.

The Met batter leading off, a big Number Four on his back, struck out. So did the next batter, Number Twenty-Two. And the fans roared on. A great vast disappointing boo of noise. And then the miracle began to unfold. And Keith Partridge took a step along the dugout, reaching for his favorite bat. A long solid piece of lumber so smoothly tapered and carved. It felt like a cannon in his hands.

A third batter, Number Twenty-Seven, singled through the infield, between the third baseman and the shortstop. The ball rolled like a marble to the outfield grass. The crowd roared.

The fourth batter walked on terribly wild pitches. Four in a row and all called balls. The crowd roared even louder.

The fifth batter, noise thundering all around him, popped the first pitch to the second baseman, who amazingly dropped the ball, and so very suddenly that it was electrifying, the Mets had the bases loaded. The tying runs were on!

And Keith Partridge, the star hitting outfielder of the New York Mets was marching up to the dish, wagging a big bat over his shoulder. Formidably, ominously. To make rival players cower.

He was tall and broad-shouldered and handsome. Every inch the star athlete. Superstar, really. Hadn't he led the league in just about everything there was? Hits, doubles, triples, homers, runs scored, runs batted in and batting average? Of course, he had!

It was Keith Partridge's dream after all.

And in our dreams, all things are possible.

As they should be.

So it was that Keith Partridge stood at home plate, in the batter's box, representing the winning run in the last inning of the last game of that very sensational baseball year. He stood there, smiling, confident and the thousands of dream-like patrons bombarded the huge stadium with the sound of their homage to a very special star. Keith The Killer. Killer Keith, who murdered baseballs every day of the season. Partridge The Magnificent. Greater than Babe Ruth, even!

The dream had a perfect script.

The pitcher, a ghostly figure out there on the mound, with

three Met baserunners dancing off the sacks, taunting him, bit the heart of the plate with two singing fast balls for called strikes. And Keith stood there, disdaining to swing. And then the next three pitches were all balls and he didn't swing at those either. And now the count was three balls and two strikes and the next pitch would and could be the end of the game if Keith Partridge failed to make contact.

Would he?

Could he?

Or do dreams disappoint us too, in the end?

Perhaps, but in other dreams, not this one.

The pitcher pitched.

A ball that hummed, roared and zipped toward the plate.

Keith Partridge swung his big bat.

Poetry in motion, a synchronization of well-trained, powerful baseball muscles. A rhythmic rotation of all his poundage and intelligence and all-too-true batting eye. Partridge at the bat, indeed.

There came a tremendous explosion as his flailing bat met the round white ball. A veritable cataclysm of noise and fury.

POW!

The dream echoed and reechoed with the thunder of the drive. The ball left home plate on a rising line, arcing higher and higher and then it was seen no more. as it shot up toward the heavens, beyond all the fences into outer space and Infinity itself.

And the dream went wild.

Met baserunners scampered around the bases, legs churning, and Keith Partridge leisurely dropped his bat and began his long and slow and very victorious journey around the bases. The dream kaleidoscoped. Into a mixed-up melodious medley of faces, noises, sights and sounds, all centralized on Keith Partridge. Mom was laughing and crying all at the same time. Laurie, Danny, Christopher and Tracy were all clapping their hands, shouting, making funny faces and dancing in the aisles of the stands. The crowd had gone absolutely wild. The dream was a torrent of noise. A flood of acclaim.

The huge ball park shuddered on its foundations.

And Keith Partridge ran and ran and ran and ran about all four bases until finally he toed home plate for the eighth and winning run as the New York Mets defeated the Baltimore Orioles by a score of 8-7 for the World Championship.

And for Keith Partridge's finest moment in a big league uniform. The finest moment of any ballplayer's life in all baseball history. No World Series had ever been decided this way. At the very last second, in the do-or-die ninth with a grand slam home run. In the hometown ball park.

And the dream didn't end there.

Keith saw himself on television, in the movies, being kissed by Raquel Welch and Elizabeth Taylor and signing autographs and being chauffeured around in a Mercedes-Benz and being showered with money and contracts. And shaking hands with President Nixon and playing a game of golf with Arnold Palmer and throwing the football with Joe Namath and having a long interview with David Frost. All of it was so golden and dreamlike, Keith wanted none of it to end.

It was the perfect world, this dream.

And he was at its very core.

Something anybody would want. To be the most important man in the world. Man, not *boy*.

There is that difference, too.

So Keith Partridge's dream rolled on during the night. A self-imposed orgy of dreams come true, wishes fulfilled, every fantasy that every boy has ever had.

Something playing the guitar and singing with his mother and brothers and sisters had not brought him as yet.

But everything takes time.

Even dreams.

Even the fulfilling of them.

That would seem to take the most time of all.

But the amount of success accomplished in so short a dream that fateful night was to be the drug that would overcome Keith Partridge's thinking when he woke up in the morning.

The dream had been too good to be true.

Therefore, he would make it come true.

Or break his neck trying.

Before the Partridge Family went to sleep that night, Leo Rampkin had already put in a late phone call to Jimmy Perkins, the manager of a farm club for the major leagues. Jimmy was an old friend of Leo Rampkin's, and Leo knew he would never fret over a late call if ever it led to the discovery of baseball gold. Or ivory, as the expression goes.

Jimmy's nasal but friendly snarl growled in response to Leo's disturbing him just as he was settling down to turn in himself.

"Well, Leo, make it good. We blew a doubleheader this afternoon and I'm about ready to eat nails. What's up?"

Jimmy Perkins ate, drank and slept baseball and Leo Rampkin knew that, too. Which was why he had thought of him in the first place. Among other reasons.

"A free agent. You still having trouble with a regular centerfielder?"

"Uh huh. I may go out there myself tomorrow. Why?"

"Kid down here in Meadowville. A-1 all down the line. He's only seventeen and still growing but if you believe in reincarnation and sometimes I do—this is another budding Hall of Famer. No fooling."

There was a long pause.

When Jimmy Perkins' voice came back, it was wide-awake now and less nasal.

"Keep talking. Tell me more."

So Leo Rampkin did.

All about the golden afternoon when a slender kid named Keith Partridge had single-handedly taken one ball game apart and wrapped it up all by his lonesome. Leo did not mention the Partridge Family.

By the time he hung up, Leo Rampkin had convinced Jimmy Perkins to show up Monday night at Meadowville Diamond for a look-see at the dawning star. Perkins' club had the day off and one hundred miles wasn't a far piece for a minor league manager to travel to see a good prospect play. Perkins had been a fine shortstop himself, about twenty years ago, with the St. Louis Cardinals before retiring to take a shot at managing his own club. And ex-big league players always dream of discovering stars of the future. That kind of wish goes with the job, too.

Leo Rampkin had known that, too, before he decided to make the phone call. If he was going to get Keith Partridge to lay his guitar down for a baseball glove, he was going to need all the ammunition he could get for his war with Shirley Partridge, who he could see wasn't too keen on the idea. Fiery, shrewd Jimmy Perkins was the necessary kind of ammo. As for Leo, it was his personal opinion that anyone who had what Keith seemed to have shouldn't waste it on a musical career. The truth be told, Leo Rampkin was a hopelessly devoted baseball buff. Something he had always wanted to be—a ballplayer, but he had a trick knee that never came around the way it should have.

So it goes.

Leo Rampkin saw in Keith Partridge the ballplayer he might have become but never did.

Which partially explains his curious insistence on butting into the Partridge Family's affairs.

But only partially.

There were more sides to Leo Rampkin's character and personality than even a close observer like Laurie Partridge had spotted.

Leo Rampkin had no intention of remaining a college faculty little-frog-in-a-big-pond sort of person. No, Sir.

He did want to amount to something, too.

As Keith Partridge's personal business manager and sponsor, he too had a dream.

And he also wanted his dreams to get better all the time.

As does everybody.

Such is the nature of the human animal no matter what its intentions are. Base or high, good or bad.

Actually, Leo Rampkin was not very happy with the amount of money he was earning as a college teacher.

Very few college teachers are.

And therein lies the story.

6

BETWEEN THE INNINGS

☐ The kiosk of a subway is a hump-backed construction which suddenly looms from the surface of the ground and presto, it is there right before your eyes. It seems to abruptly be in sight. So it was with the vague and menacing shadows that Shirley Partridge had been all too aware of during Leo Rampkin's dinner visit. But the chimerical monster did not rear up in all its unwholesome and true character until a few days later. But in between the long interval of the dinner and the next appearance of Mr. Leo Rampkin on the scene, there were some glaring and unmistakable signs; the kind one tries to ignore but cannot because they will not go away and remain to plague the heart and brain anew.

For one thing, there was the strange behavior of Keith Partridge to contend with.

Something very new had been added to his character. And temperament and personality.

For one thing, he disappeared right after Sunday church services and Shirley didn't see him until much later that afternoon. Before she could even ask him what he was up to, he vanished up the carpeted stairway beyond the front hall and disappeared into his bedroom. She was curiously aware of the large brown package he had tucked under his left arm. Not that he was hiding it from her but he made no mention of it at all. Which was strange in itself. Keith was not the sort of a boy to do anything furtive.

Shirley wondered about the package all that afternoon as she took care of some mail and prepared supper. The rest of the kids busied themselves at their various hobbies and diversions. Laurie, with typical teenage tyranny, monopolized the telephone most of that day, calling all her chums to discuss the merits of boys, movies, civil rights, and particularly, Leo Rampkin, with them. Danny buried his keen nose in a copy of *The Wall Street Journal* and made some computations on a long yellow ruled pad. Christopher developed an interest in an old John Wayne western on TV that was full of Indians and cavalrymen and the aforementioned Mr. Wayne. Tracy, who like most little girls just couldn't stand horse operas, played with the new doll house which Reuben Kinkaid had presented to her on her last birthday.

And Keith stayed in his room and didn't come down.

Until the mystery of his silence was too much for Shirley Partridge, who took one last look at the turkey in the oven, wiped her hands off on her apron, and trotted upstairs to see what was cooking with her Number One Son.

The door of his room was closed and since she had always taught her children to respect the privacy of the individual, she politely knocked on the door.

"Come in, it's open," Keith's voice called out. Motherlike, Shirley Partridge could read nothing portentous or different in the tone of her son's voice. She strolled into the room as casually as she could make it. There was such a thing as *overdoing* the mother role.

Whatever she had expected, it was not to be learned from looking at Keith. He was lying sprawled on his bed, staring up at the ceiling, arms folded behind his head. Shirley's eyes raced over the room; the floor, walls, closet, chairs, desk, table, framed pictures. There was no sight of the mysterious brown package.

She had always liked Keith's room. He wasn't the ordinary teenage boy. He *did* make up his bed and neatly hung up his clothes at all times. The only untidy thing in the room was the careless way he always kicked his shoes off. Even now, one discarded loafer was lying in the doorway, its brown leather mate clear over on the other side of the bed, under the curtained window.

"Hi. Whatcha doin'?"

"Hi, Mom. Nothing."

"You must be doing something," she said, lightly, sitting on the bed, next to his long legs. "You're frowning and its putting wrinkles in your forehead."

"Well—I have been thinking."

"That's what I thought. Want to talk about it?"

He didn't answer right away and she waited, without urging him, carefully plucking a loose black thread from the sock of his left foot.

"Mom?"

"Yes, honey?"

"You remember what Leo Rampkin was talking about at dinner? You know—me maybe going out for baseball?"

"Of course, I remember. You must have been really terrific in that game. He carried on so. You really impressed him and he didn't strike me as a fool who goes overboard without giving it a lot of thought. I wish I'd been there, Keith. It would have made me so proud."

He heaved a long sigh.

"Yeah, it was really something, even if I do say so myself. I can't tell you how good it made me feel."

She chuckled softly, patting his knee, keeping the uneasiness out of her voice. The uneasiness that was struggling to come alive again in all its glory.

"So I can imagine. So what do you want to tell me?"

He took a beat and then slowly, his eyes still on the ceiling, he quietly said: "I'm thinking of giving it a whirl." Just like that. Had he blurted, or gushed, or apologized, she might have been able to combat the decision with some no-nos or advice or opinions. But so forcefully and firmly did he state his case that for a very long moment she was incapable of saying anything.

Her mind was flying and her heart was bumping and inwardly, she felt a bit ridiculous. Her boy wanted to be a baseball player—it wasn't as if he was telling her he wanted to go to Vietnam or that he wanted to be a cardsharp gambler. Or a bum. After all, when you're growing into a man, like Keith certainly was, there are decisions. And there are decisions.

"I see," she finally said. "Which means you'll be going to Meadowville Diamond tomorrow night to play in that game."

"Uh huh. That's the whole idea. I want to see if the great game I had was a fluke. If I strike out a few times and drop a

55

couple of flyballs, well—" He laughed. "Anyhow, I'd like to try. If it's all right with you."

She loved him for saying that. She would have hugged him right then and there but it would have dissolved her into tears and solved nothing. So she simply locked her fingers together, placed her hands around her knees and stared down at her son. He wasn't looking at the ceiling anymore. His eyes were riveted on her face, waiting for her answer. Shirley Partridge cleared her throat.

"Keith, listen to me."

"I'm listening, Mom."

"Anything you do is all right with me. You know that. You're my son and I'll always be proud of you because you've always given me good reason to be proud of you. You're a decent, intelligent boy and your heart's always been in the right place—your father loved you for those qualities just as I do. We've always talked things over. Like the time you smacked up the car learning to drive, and the first time you threw a rock at a store window. So we'll talk now. About this. Because it's important and because I love you."

"Hey—" he said sharply, sitting up suddenly. "Don't cry."

"I am *not* crying," she sniffled, brushing at her eyes. "And if I am, it's a perfectly natural thing, isn't it?"

"Well—uh—yeah," he said, sheepishly.

"Good," she snapped. "Glad we got that cleared up. Now about your decision to see whether or not you could be a major league ballplayer, there are one or two objections, right off the bat."

He looked puzzled. "Such as?"

She controlled herself and plunged on.

"*One*—we play the Twilight Room in a short time. A very important, very lucrative engagement. One that puts the bread on the table and allows us to live fairly pleasantly. Right or wrong?"

"Right but—"

"Please let me finish. I'd love it if you became a baseball star, *someday*, let's say, but right now, suppose you were to injure either of your hands—you know, break a finger, your wrist or something worse—what would happen to the Twilight Room date? You realize we'd have to cancel, and you know what that means—we'd probably never be asked back there again."

56

"Oh, Mom."

"Oh Mom what?"

"I'm not going to hurt myself. Besides, even if it did happen, you and the kids could put on the act without me. Nobody's indispensable."

"You are to me," she said, firmly. "And we could put on the act but we wouldn't be as good without you. And that's the truth, not just something to make you feel good."

"Oh, Mom." He was sheepish, now.

But she wasn't done with him yet.

"And *two*," she said with added emphasis. "You have to practice to be a ballplayer. Right? And you have to rehearse to be a musician. A lot of practicing and a lot of rehearsing if you're going to be fairly expert and professional at either. Now—how can you find the time for both?"

He bit his lower lip and an intent light gleamed from his eyes. Then he shrugged.

"I could do both. I'm sure of it. Anyhow, lately, I haven't been that keen about the guitar—"

She was shocked.

She stared down at him.

"Now *that* . . . that is *news* to me. Since when? You love the guitar. You love music. Ever since you wiggled your baby toes. You're the one who got us interested in Hi-Fi and Stereo and got your father to convert the garage into a recording studio. You're the one who dropped all other things—even baseball games—so you could fool around with your guitar and play all day long. Keith Partridge, I'm amazed to hear something so . . . well, profane from you. You're the one who's responsible for Laurie and Danny and Christopher and Tracy being so musically hip. And you mean to sit there and tell me you're not so keen about the guitar? Keith, you've been bewitched. The ball game must have been something, all right. It's made you lose your sense of perspective!"

"Mom, you just don't understand."

"Oh, yes, I do. You let the applause foul you up. It went to your head and now you're dreaming big things. Keith, I want you to be anything you want. You know that. But you are a fine musician and you'll be even better someday. I can't let you throw that away for a lark—"

The unfortunate word was out of her mouth before she could stop it. She regretted it as soon as she said it. Because

57

his expression went grim and cold and something strange lit up his eyes. He turned away from her and faced the far wall. As if he didn't want to look at her.

"It is *not* a lark," he said.

"Keith, I'm sorry—"

"No, you're not. You think I'm silly. To want to be something else besides a musician. You're prejudiced, Mom. And I'm surprised at you. I guess you think it's silly for me to want to make a hundred thousand dollars a year. To be on my own. And not part of a family act. Well, maybe I am silly. But I do want to try it."

His back was to her and she wanted to touch him but she didn't. She got off the bed, flattened her palms against her apron and felt defeat flooding her. The first time she really discussed his new love with him and she'd blown it! What a goof-up.

She couldn't repair the damage in a hurry. She was wise enough to spot that, too. So she retreated toward the bedroom door, leaving him still on the bed, brooding and hurt.

"Honey, we'll talk about it more after dinner. Okay? I have to see about the turkey."

"Sure," he said, sulking.

"Don't be mad. Please?"

"I'm not mad."

"You sound mad."

"I don't mean to. I'm sorry."

"I'm sorry, too. Well, see you later—"

He murmured something and she left the room.

She was behind the door, with the portal closed between them, when she realized she still hadn't discovered the contents of the big brown package. Though she had a few guesses up her sleeve, by now.

The way Keith had carried on she wouldn't have been at all surprised to learn that he had gone out and purchased one big league uniform complete. With *The New York Mets* stitched across the chest. Baseball had come late to Keith Partridge, but judging by the tenor of his talk, it had most certainly *come!*

Perturbed and unhappy, Shirley Partridge walked slowly down the stairway toward her large and shining kitchen to see about the fifteen pound turkey cooking for dinner.

At that precise moment in her life, she felt as bad off as the poor turkey.

She didn't seem to have much to be thankful for, either.
Not just then, at any rate.

After his mother left the room, Keith Partridge glared at the door. For one of the very few times in his life, he felt a fine flash of dislike for Shirley Partridge. But it was fleeting and almost ephemeral. It was gone in an instant.

Rather than dwell on something so strange, he jumped off the bed and hurried to the bedroom closet. Pulling the door back, he dug for a second and then drew forth the brown package he had brought home from downtown Meadowville. Though the package bore no markings of any kind, Keith had in actuality made some purchases at the local Sporting Goods Shop, Mr. Tompkins' fine store which had been in business as long as Keith could remember. Shirley Partridge had bought his first pair of ice skates there.

But it wasn't ice skates that Keith had brought home this time.

He placed the package carefully on the bed, having postponed the moment of unveiling, while he thought things over for a long time. But now he didn't have to wait anymore. The die was cast.

His mind was made up.

If he'd had any doubts or second thoughts or other considerations, Mom had helped him make up his mind.

As women usually did. Sooner or later.

Breathing slowly, Keith, his eyes shining with expectancy, undid the taped wrappings of the parcel. He quickly pulled the paper apart and his fingers dug hungrily.

Soon, his purchase at Mr. Tompkins' store lay exposed on the bed. It was late afternoon and there was no electric light turned on but enough daylight filtered through the window.

Enough illumination to show a heterogeneous assortment of sporting goods. All of them of a piece. All of them in the same class.

An assortment which included:

One baseball glove, outfielder's model, major league brand.
One baseball, the official, authorized 1970 kind.
One blue, peaked, baseball cap, with red piping.
And about a half-dozen books and magazines all devoted and dedicated to the great American National Pastime—Baseball.

Shirley Partridge had scored one hundred percent in the guessing league.

Well, almost one hundred percent.

Laurie Partridge was still riveted to the pink telephone in her bedroom. She had had a most interesting afternoon talking to her teenage girl chums. It was exciting and fascinating the different things you could converse about—all on one phone. The exchange of ideas and notions and dreams with other girls your own age was groovy.

And neat-o!

What was even more rewarding and a personal triumph for her was that mention of Leo Rampkin's name set off bells in all the other girls. The fact that Laurie had had such a prize as a house guest for dinner had made her the belle of the ball. To a girl each of Laurie's chums thought Leo Rampkin was "gorgeous" and a prize beyond compare. The Perfect Man.

So Laurie drew to the close of her telephone marathon —she had already talked to about seven eagerly listening pals —feeling supremely content and happy. Mom had shouted up the stairs that dinner was almost ready. Laurie, winding up her talk with Belle Ballantine, sighed into the transmitter and unwrapped her long legs, probing without looking, for her sandals on the floor by her bed.

"—well, gotta split, Belle. But show up at the Diamond tomorrow night. Sure now, huh?"

"Wouldn't miss it for the world," Belle answered, fervently. "I'd like to see just how much Leo Rampkin likes you."

Laurie smiled triumphantly.

Belle was a beautiful, slender brunette whose father was the Number One banker in Meadowville. And quite a girl, all in all. She and Laurie had been natural rivals. In everything from Spelling Bees to Dancing Contests. Which was why Laurie had saved talking to her until last. To savor her apparent victory all the more.

"Come and see, girl. And you will see."

"Bye, Laurie. I'll be there."

Laurie Partridge cradled the phone, humming under her breath.

The second bit of trouble which was to plague Shirley Partridge's maternal life was now well underway, too.

Two bits of hectic strife which were to considerably undermine the present and future of the Partridge Family.

Reuben Kinkaid, bless his acumen, had always been on record as saying: *"A widow with five growing children can get in all kinds of trouble if left to her own devices long enough."*

Kinkaid, to paraphrase General William Tecumseh Sherman, was right.

Widowhood is hell.

A woman does need a man around the house for just such emergencies as starry-eyed sons and love-sick daughters.

Ask any mother.

7

MONDAY MADNESS

☐ Baseball is a funny game, as Joe Garagiola once said in his funny book about the National Pastime. But Shirley Partridge found nothing very laughable about the Monday night contest at Meadowville Diamond.

Wisely, she had chosen to attend, wanting Keith to know and understand that her motherly protest about his career ideas did not include staying away from a ball game in which her son might play. The rest of the family went too. As though it were some very special night. And all of them seemed to find some perverse pleasure in dressing up for the occasion exactly as if it were a Red Letter Day in the history of the Partridge Family.

For starters, Laurie went to town on her wardrobe for the evening. Never had Shirley seen her daughter dressed to the nines for something so casual as a night game.

A miniskirt of powder blue rayon, a very becoming necklace of love beads, a red ribbon in her long blonde hair and young Laurie looked like a debutante ready for her coming-out party.

Danny Partridge wore, surprisingly enough, a sportcoat of pure Madras colors, cream-white slacks, black loafers and his red hair for once was tidily combed.

Christopher and Tracy, not to be outdone, had put on their

Sunday best. Chris was togged out in his sober blue two-button suit and little Tracy was a dream in her two-piece beige outfit with picture hat to match.

Completely at a loss to understand all this dressing up, Shirley gave in to the situation and put on one of her best dresses. A Susan Street model; sleeveless green sheath dress which accented her trim figure and set off her blonde hair and peaches and cream complexion. It seemed ridiculous somehow to dress up so well for sports.

The topper was Keith Partridge himself.

It was like some conspiracy, the whole family attending a ball game to which Leo Rampkin had invited him, but when they all piled into the family car—a light blue stationwagon—Keith's apparel was the last straw.

The peaked blue baseball cap with the red piping rode jauntily on his head. His old high school jersey encased his torso and his feet were rammed into the regulation spiked shoes all ballplayers must wear. But he said nothing to Shirley Partridge as he took his seat next to her at the wheel. She didn't have to ask him anything anyway. The expectant glint in his eyes and the set of his chin were two formidable weapons.

Shirley Partridge sighed, feeling the situation was somehow escaping her control. She had had a very sleepless night wondering how to cope with this new aspect of her son's life. In the end, she had decided to do nothing. Not just yet, anyway. A lot of things could happen in one ball game to change Keith's way of thinking.

Like maybe striking out four times in a row or making the error that cost the old ball game?

"Everybody got their seat belts fastened?" she sang out from force of habit.

There was a chorus of assent and some tardy scrambling to do as she instructed. Tracy always took the longest to put hers on unless Christopher helped her.

It was six-thirty, the family had had an early supper and the ball game was scheduled for eight o'clock. Meadowville Diamond was no more than a fifteen minute ride from the house. Shirley knew that Keith had phoned Leo Rampkin in the interim between Sunday dinner and now and had asked to be put in the lineup for the game. The six o'clock batting practice suggestion had been a ruse on Leo's part to get Keith to bite. And bite he had. Leo had scored a direct hit. Word had come that Keith Partridge would be the starting centerfielder for the Meadowville Hawks versus the Todd Center Owls. It was just a traditional game—no league contest or anything like that—and Keith the Partridge was to be a Hawk for one night. Leo Rampkin's plan was going along without a hitch, so far.

Shirley Partridge drove at forty miles an hour toward the big, rambling old ball park on the outskirts of town. The Meadowville Diamond had been in existence since 1901 and the legend still persisted in town that Ty Cobb had once played there on a Sunday afternoon when the Detroit Tigers had stopped over in Meadowville because of a storm delay on the railroad. According to local oldtimers, who liked to spin yarns around the soda fountain in Murphy's Drug Emporium and The English Inn on Grove Street, Cobb had hit a home run and stolen three bases on that long ago afternoon, just having fun with the Meadowville team of that era. It might all have been a lie but it was a pleasant bit of Meadowville history to play around with.

Or so Shirley Partridge had always thought until now.

"Keith," Tracy piped up from the back seat where she was staring at the back of her oldest brother's head. "You going to hit a homer for me tonight? I'd like that."

"I'd like it too, Tracy," Keith laughed. "But it isn't so easy to hit home runs."

"But you can try, can't you?"

"I promise. I'll try."

That seemed to satisfy her.

"Good." She settled back in her seat, content. "If Keith hits a homer then, it's all mine."

Christopher snorted, scowling at her.

"You're a little girl, you know that?"

Now, Shirley laughed.

"Of course she's a little girl. She's not a giraffe or an Eskimo. You children—" She shook her head.

Laurie Partridge, acutely aware of her own dressiness, her mind full of pictures of Belle Ballantine stewing in her own juices when she saw Leo Rampkin in Laurie's company, was paying no attention to the talk at all. Keith's important game was just a means to an end, as far as Laurie was concerned. And the end was Leo Rampkin, handsome, groovy Leo.

All the girls were going to flip and turn green with envy when they saw the rapport she was going to have with Leo Rampkin.

Danny Partridge, at the other extreme, was completely engulfed in his brother's potential emergence as a baseball headliner. That was pretty obvious, too, in Shirley Partridge's awareness. Little Danny, the financial whiz, had been mentally counting dollar bills since Sunday. He had what Shirley thought of as the Reuben Kinkaid Syndrome. *Money, money, money!*

"You gotta be great tonight, Keith," Danny said very seriously. "So lay off any curve balls this guy might throw at you and swing only at the fast balls. And then only—I repeat *only*—when they're over the plate."

Keith's head swung around and he glared at Danny.

"Since when are you the baseball expert?"

"Since right now." Danny did not take offense. He never did because he always knew his facts. "I read Ted Williams' book on hitting and he knows what he's talking about. Besides, it's just common sense. Curve balls are hard to hit whereas fast balls—"

"Oh, shut up," Keith said and faced the front again.

"Now, boys—" Shirley began, making the peace, as usual.

"Then tell Big Brain to knock it off," Keith snapped.

"Danny, simmer down. You'll upset your brother. After all, he could be a little nervous going out to play a game that's important to him."

"That's just the point, Mom," Danny persisted. "It *is* important. Important to all we Partridges. Do you realize Keith could be a real big star someday?"

"He's a star right now," Shirley sighed. "You all are. And I wish you would all remember how we earn our living. We are musicians and after this outing, I'm going to crack down on all of you. Rehearsals are going to be the first order of the day at Partridge House. We need to practice before we can think of going into a big place like the Twilight Room, don't we? Sure we do! So we'll all have a relaxing evening watching Keith play ball. But come tomorrow, I'm going to be a regular Simon Legree. We need to polish up the act. But definitely."

"We'll practice," Danny agreed loftily. "But you must realize, Mom, what is at stake tonight."

"Oh, dry up, Danny," Keith said in a low voice. Which

showed that he was disturbed. So Danny shrugged, folded his arms, and looked out the car window at the tall trees flashing by in waves of beautiful, shadowy green. Early evening dusk was beginning to settle over everything growing. Laurie Partridge, caught up in a vision of herself and Leo Rampkin holding hands at the game while Belle Ballantine fumed, was oblivious of all that was going on about her.

"Almost there," Shirley said as she turned the car into the long stretch of gravel leading toward the big old ball park beyond the trees.

"Not soon enough for me," Keith Partridge said in a funny voice. The glint in his eye had returned.

Shirley Partridge somehow didn't like the sound of his voice.

It was so cold, so hard. So much, well—*older*.

As if the latent man in the growing boy had suddenly peered out from under several layers of skin. It was the sound of a comparative stranger. Someone she really didn't know.

She restrained a shudder as she aimed the stationwagon for the uneven rows of parked vehicles before her. It looked like a big crowd was showing up for the old ball game.

She had never thought the sport of baseball could ever be capable of producing a sense of apprehension over her bones.

It was so silly, really!

Still—it was unnerving.

Jimmy Perkins was about fifty years old but even as Leo Rampkin found him sitting intently in the stands along the first base line, squinting out at the players warming up, it wasn't possible to assess his true age. Perkins could have passed for a man in his very late thirties. Mainly because he was still lean and trim and the grey at his temples and the perennial ballplayer's tan combined to give him that peculiar appearance of distinguished alertness that some men are blessed with. In any case, Leo had no trouble finding him. Perkins was firmly entrenched in his seat, his eyes nowhere else but on the field. The park was filling up rapidly as game time was drawing near.

"Hi, Jimmy. Glad you could make it."

"After what you told me on the phone, I'd be a chump not to."

"You won't be wasting your time. You'll see."

"You're a smart young boy, Leo," Jimmy Perkins grunted,

still watching the field with its players running, throwing and batting. "It's always worth a little effort if you can find a star in the sticks. Which one's Partridge?"

Leo Rampkin scanned the field. He smiled.

"Number Seventeen. The pepper game at third and short."

Jimmy Perkins squinted in the designated direction. He saw Keith Partridge, wiry and graceful, having a spirited catch with one of the other players. Behind him, in the third base side seats, Shirley Partridge and the family were conspicuously forming a rooting section of five. Leo had made sure they had gotten very good seats.

Perkins scowled. "Kind of a lightweight, isn't he?"

"He'll fool you," Leo averred, still convinced of Keith's ability. "Lot of power at the plate. Wait and see."

"That's what I'm here for," Perkins agreed. "But he sure doesn't look like much from here."

"He's a growing boy, Jimmy. And he'll keep on growing."

"Uh huh," said Jimmy Perkins. "So let's get this show on the road."

It was as if someone had heard him. No sooner had the words left his lips than a tall man in blue marched up to home plate, whisked a hand broom over the dish and boomed in a very loud voice, "PLAY BALL!"

The Meadowville Hawks, as the home team which would bat last only if they had to, swooped out to take the field. The Todd Center Owls had first at bat. It was all very informal, with very little ceremony, but the people filling the stands cut loose with an ovation that would have done credit to the opening game of a World Series.

Keith Partridge ran quickly out to center field and took up his position. It was where Leo Rampkin had wanted him to play that night, knowing Jimmy Perkins' desperate need.

The ex-major leaguer's club in Cedar Rapids needed a slugging right-hand hitting outfielder very badly. Leo knew that. Leo also knew that if Keith Partridge filled the bill, his first step in his master plan to get his hands on some big money would be well underway.

Shirley Partridge, sitting behind the third base line, of course, knew nothing of Leo Rampkin's long-range scheme. To all appearances, her biggest concern was Keith getting over his baseball fever in time for the important engagement at the Twilight Room.

She never would have guessed about Leo Rampkin.

68

In fact, the only problem that Leo seemed to present was Laurie Partridge's blooming interest in him. Shirley could tell how Laurie preened and fluttered when Leo had shown them to their seats. She was not unaware of the fuming Belle Ballantine, radiant and beautiful in her seat no more than ten removed from the Partridge Family.

Like all mothers the world over, Shirley was convinced that everything did pass in time. And with time. Time cured everything. From budding ballplayers to teenage romances.

Nothing stayed the same, really.

Including your growing children.

She was sure of that. Or so she tried to tell herself.

But she couldn't help worrying.

And when the first Owl batter swung at the first pitch and lo and behold it flew out toward center field like a rocket, she felt her heart jump right up to her mouth and skip a beat. The stands came alive with noise. The ball kept on going.

And where was Keith Partridge?

The kids, Laurie, Danny, Christopher and Tracy, were all shouting like a Greek Chorus and Shirley was almost afraid to look. It was a new experience for her. Motherly tension at a ball game because her own son just happened to be playing. She didn't know how to feel!

Despairingly, longingly, she made herself follow the flight of the ball.

Out toward center field where Keith Partridge suddenly loomed into view, running at top speed, like a madman. He lost his cap somewhere on his desperate race.

It didn't seem very possible that he could catch up with the ball.

8

A STAR AT NIGHT

☐ No, it didn't seem possible—but he did.

Never at any time would Shirley Partridge have been able to recount or describe how her son caught that ball.

One second he was nowhere in sight, the climbing baseball soaring for the center field fence. Then a fleeting moment later, a blur of racing uniform, a gazellelike spring into the air. And the ball came down at the base of the wall with Keith clutching it very deftly in his outstretched glove. Without a single scintilla of loss of grace or awkward motion.

The park shuddered with thunderous applause and all about the Partridge Family sounded hoarse and ringing shouts of acclaim and awe.

"What did I tell you?" Danny crowed. "A star!"

"Attaboy, Keith!" Laurie shrieked.

"Wowwee!" Christopher cried.

"That's my brother," Tracy told anyone that would listen.

"Not bad," Shirley murmured in a dazed voice. "Not bad at all." She still couldn't understand how he had ever caught up with a ball traveling so far and so high and so fast.

From his first base seat, Jimmy Perkins squinted even deeper as Leo Rampkin nudged him in the side, forcibly.

"Sure covers a lot of ground," Jimmy Perkins ventured.

Leo Rampkin chuckled happily.

Shirley Partridge found herself trembling weirdly and not knowing why. Seeing her son in a different light and a newer and yes! somehow more wonderful role had done something to her. But it was only the beginning. She had no way of knowing that the Lord was moving in even more mysterious ways his wonders to perform.

Or rather, maybe Keith Partridge was.

The game was scoreless in the bottom of the first and Keith came up with two out and nobody on base. The crowd gave him a big hand for his circus catch in the outfield. Keith responded in classic fashion. With the count two balls and one strike, he slammed the next pitch with line drive ferocity, pulling the ball down the line. But only up, up, up and over the low barrier beyond the leftfielder. Nobody caught that ball. It cleared the wall by a good five feet. As Keith circled the bases with the Hawks' first run, Shirley Partridge kept shaking her head. She was experiencing the wonderful dream that Keith had had Sunday night. When everything had come up roses.

Again, the kids roared their sibling approval.

Again, Leo Rampkin prodded Jimmy Perkins.

Again, Perkins squinted, his eyes slitting as though he was impressed.

"Good clout," he muttered. "Considering the wind is blowing to right tonight."

Leo Rampkin smiled the smile the cat smiles when the canary flies innocently and happily out of the cage.

And the game throbbed on, complete with everything that Leo Rampkin wanted, and all that Shirley Partridge did not know how to accept. It wasn't easy to see with your own eyes the sudden emergence of a diamond star who up until that night, in her eyes at least, had only been a bright, lovable boy who could play a mean guitar and sing a professional brand of music.

To Laurie Partridge, sulking a bit because Leo Rampkin was spending all his time with Jimmy Perkins and fuming inwardly because Belle Ballantine must be giving her the horse laugh, the game was a torment of sorts. Leo was spoiling it all by sitting somewhere else. It was more galling because he had said hello so nicely before game time, seeming genuinely glad to see her again. But the rest of the Partridges were reveling in Keith Partridge's big night.

And so it was. Like Sunday's fantastic game all over again. Keith was having another game to remember.

Following his homer in the bottom half of the first inning, he tripled into the right field corner on his next turn at bat and this led to a big inning for the Hawks. By mid-game, they were ahead of the Owls 7-0. The hometown crowd ate it all up, too. Along with a lot of hot dogs and Cokes and popcorn.

In the next inning, Keith made a shoestring catch, ranging far over from center into short right field to cut off a big Owl rally. When he came in from his position at the inning's end, he received a two-minute ovation. Even Jimmy Perkins ungrudgingly applauded that one. The squint was gone from his eyes, altogether. Jimmy Perkins knew exactly what he was bearing witness to, now.

That rarest of all athletes—the *natural* ballplayer.

There didn't seem to be a thing that Keith Partridge needed to be taught. Only time and experience were necessary to mature the gifts he so very obviously had.

By inning eight if he had any doubts at all, they were banished forever. The Partridge boy came up with runners at first and third and without hardly batting an eye in such a spot, deftly bunted the ball halfway between third and home. A great bunt. A thing of beauty. The man on third scored, Keith had a single for his third hit—he had walked on four straight pitches earlier—and the Hawks were murdering the Owls 10-0. The result of the game was a foregone conclusion.

Jimmy Perkins had made up his mind.

Quickly, unalterably.

If this Partridge kid wasn't another natural like Mel Ott and Mickey Mantle and Mays—then he didn't know the first thing about baseball.

As the Owls harmlessly were going down in the ninth, one, two, three, Jimmy Perkins turned to a triumphant Leo Rampkin and nodded.

"I want him."

"Knew you would, Jimmy."

"So how do we get him?"

Leo nodded, too.

"You'll have to talk to him. I think he wants to be a ballplayer. But there is a problem."

73

Jimmy Perkins winced sourly. Suspiciously.

"Such as?"

Leo Rampkin took a deep breath and committed himself, all the way. Jimmy would have to know sooner or later. Sooner was better.

"Keith Partridge is one of the Partridge Family. Don't know whether or not you follow the music world, but he's already a star in the music field. The Partridge Family has made quite a name for itself already—and it's getting to be a bigger name all the time."

Perkins glowered.

"Now he tells me."

"Would you have come if I told you that first?"

"Who's got the time?" Perkins growled acidly. "But now that I've seen what he can do—" He shrugged, a mixture of victory and defeat. Leo leaned toward him, completely ignoring Laurie Partridge, who had squeezed out of her seat and was standing up, waving her hand to catch his attention. Jimmy Perkins laughed before he answered Leo's next question: "Now that you've seen him, Jimmy?" It was almost a goad.

"A kid who can play this game like that," Perkins said with considerable vehemence, "has no business doing something else. Or being something else."

Leo Rampkin sighed and sat back.

"I was hoping you'd feel like that," he said.

"There's no other way for me to feel, Leo. Baseball needs all the stars it can get."

Fittingly and almost poetically, Keith Partridge made the last putout of the game. The final Owl batter lofted a lazy flyball to short center. Keith trotted in, camped under it, gloved it and the ball park erupted with enthusiastic partisanship. The home team had solidly been in command all the way and the score of 10-0 was a one-sided display of hometown superiority. A truly murderous score to win by.

Something to talk about in the long winter months to come.

Something to shout about.

Also, the whole night, like the Sunday game, had the same aura of freshness and newness about it. The night a star was born. Keith Partridge, slugging center fielder of the Meadowville Hawks.

74

And this particular Hawk had flown high, wide and handsome.

A pretty good stunt considering he was a Partridge to begin with.

Shirley Partridge, at turns gloriously happy and woefully miserable, didn't know how to gauge her true feelings and emotions.

She had gained an outfielder, all right, but she may have lost a son in the process. The poor mother was bewildered.

And didn't know how to behave, really.

Whatever Keith would eventually be in this world, she needed him most urgently as the eldest and most valuable of the act known as the Partridge Family. Without him, playing the Twilight Room was just not possible. Playing anywhere without him wasn't possible.

She began to cry, the unbidden tears poised on her eyelids. As Keith walked over to join the family, acknowledging the tributes of the people around him, a big smile on his face, Shirley Partridge was fighting the battle of mixed emotions. And losing badly.

Her pride was at war with her brain.

But you would never have known it to look at her.

Nor been able to tell by what she said.

"Keith, you were—marvelous. I'm so proud."

"Thanks, Mom. Did you enjoy the game?"

Danny, Christopher and Tracy were crowding around him, slapping him all over the body, trying to get their kudos in first.

"Sure I enjoyed it," Shirley Partridge smiled through her tears. "You practically won the game all by your lonesome. You were the star!"

His face broke, confused.

"Then why are you crying?"

"Because I'm happy, silly. You know I always cry when I'm happy. I'm not made of stone, you know."

"No," he said, kissing her damp cheek. "You sure aren't. You're just about the mushiest person I know, you know that?"

"You, young sir," she said with mock severity, "will kindly shut up and go take your shower or whatever it is you ballplayers do and the kids and I will meet you in the parking lot. That is if you can dodge signing a lot of autographs from your many admirers, Mr. Partridge."

"Sure thing, Mom. Give me about twenty minutes—"

All about them, the crowd milled and murmured and pointed. Admiringly. Shirley smiled bravely through it all. But deep in her heart, the same old tension picked up again. She felt as if she was being put through a wringer of some kind. One not of her own making. She had been caught totally unprepared.

And then she spotted Leo Rampkin in the sea of faces. Leo coming toward her and Laurie springing to meet him. But Leo dodged her expertly and now Shirley could see the tall, sun-tanned man with him. A man who looked like an athlete and that very authoritative manner of bearing made Shirley Partridge's uneasiness several degrees deeper.

"Mrs. Partridge, Shirley—" Leo Rampkin was saying in a peculiar kind of voice. "This is somebody I want you to meet. Jimmy Perkins. Jimmy manages a Class A team in the Western League and—"

The words were innocuous, pleasant and in no way offensive but to Shirley Partridge, each and every syllable was like a litany of disaster. Like a judgment of doom from a justice on the bench.

Like an announcement that somehow would take her son from her.

It made her oddly cold, all over.

While Jimmy Perkins engaged Shirley Partridge in an animated discussion, Leo Rampkin allowed himself to be led off to one side by Laurie Partridge. Laurie, sure of her impact and the attractiveness of her appearance, wanted to be quite certain that Belle Ballantine and any of the other girls who were watching would drink the entire scene in. After all, what was the sense of rigging yourself up like a movie star if you didn't get some good out of it.

"Have you been avoiding me, Leo Rampkin?"

"How could I?"

"Well, I waved to you a couple of times but you were so busy with that gray-haired man, I began to wonder."

"Don't wonder. That's Jimmy Perkins and I brought him down here to see Keith do his stuff."

Laurie wrinkled her nose. "Whatever for?"

Leo Rampkin laughed.

"We've been over this before, I think. Your brother has the potential to be a great baseball player."

Laurie's eyes widened in amazement.

"Leo! You didn't!"

It was Leo's turn to look surprised.

"Didn't what?"

"Get a talent scout or something to come down to see Keith. Mom wouldn't like that. Don't you realize how much the Partridges need Keith as part of the act?"

Leo stiffened as if she had poked him with her finger.

"Isn't Keith old enough to make his own decisions about what he wants to do with his life?"

"Of course, he is," Laurie snapped, forgetting for a moment her plans to attract Leo Rampkin with honey. "But he doesn't have to be shoved either. He ought to be able to make up his own mind."

"I hope he will," Leo said, keeping one eye on Jimmy Perkins and Shirley Partridge in up-close discussion. The other Partridges were fidgeting, restless to leave the park. But Shirley Partridge looked very determined about something. Leo began to worry. "If Keith can be greater in another field, well, your Mom ought to let him go."

Laurie eyed him suspiciously.

"Why are you so interested in what my brother might become?"

Leo coughed.

"Well, I like him for one thing. For another, he just has it in him to be a really great ballplayer. You ask Jimmy Perkins. He was a great star himself and he knows if anybody does."

"I just might do that," Laurie said, a trifle sadly, realizing very suddenly that gorgeous Leo's interest in the Partridge Family did not go very much beyond Keith Partridge.

"Well, hello—" a voice behind them abruptly called. A voice oozing with sex appeal, lyrical smoothness and honeyed tones. Laurie gritted her teeth and repressed a groan. Belle Ballantine had come slithering down from her seat. Leo Rampkin turned to look at her and Laurie did not like the way his eyes opened wide with a flicker of new interest. She had to admit that Belle Ballantine looked simply marvelous. With her long black hair as sleek as velvet, her checkered culottes and tawny skin. And those darn even white teeth of hers!

She made the introductions, choking on them.

"Leo, this is Belle Ballantine. Leo Rampkin . . ."

"Very pleased to meet you, Belle."

77

"Charmed, Leo."

"Did you enjoy the game?"

"Marvelous. So exciting. And Keith is a favorite of mine . . ."

Laurie Partridge closed her eyes, slowly dying inside.

She knew how Belle Ballantine operated. She could see that Leo was already nibbling at the bait. Belle had picked off just about all the available males in Meadowville. And it looked like even Leo Rampkin wasn't going to be any different from anybody else.

Leo Rampkin whom she had had such high hopes for.

Darn all men anyway.

The night had hardly begun and Belle Ballantine was ruining it right off the bat.

As well as Keith with his grandstand playing.

"I'll have to think about it, Mr. Perkins," Shirley Partridge finally concluded her talk with the tall, graying athlete who had opened her eyes about the potential of her son.

"You do that, Mrs. Partridge. You have my card. Call me as soon as the boy decides. I'd give a lot to be able to use him in the last month of the season. We make our run for the pennant then."

She smiled thinly, wishing she could agree with this nice, sincere man that a teenager like Keith should be a ballplayer and nothing else. Perkins had wisely stayed away from Keith altogether, choosing to work on the mother first. Out of courtesy, out of shrewd, bargaining experience. He could see Mom Partridge already had her doubts and he had merely redoubled them. Which was good.

"Yes, I'll call. But Keith and I have always talked things over. We'll certainly have to talk this one out. I just wish you weren't so positive he was so very outstanding."

"He is, Mrs. Partridge," Jimmy Perkins averred devoutly. "I'd stake my career in baseball on it. Kid his size who hits the way he does can only get better. He could always play the guitar in the off-season. Lots of ballplayers do."

"We'll see. Well, thank you for your interest."

"Thank *you*, Mrs. Partridge."

Jimmy Perkins vanished into the departing crowd. Not much later, Keith emerged from the stands, freshly showered, hair combed and shining like a million dollars. Shirley wearily rounded up the family, including a strangely silent and moody Laurie, and suggested they all return to the station-wagon where they would decide to go for a victory celebration of Keith's big night.

"Where's Leo?" Shirley asked Laurie.

"I don't know. And I don't care."

"Oh. Like that, huh?"

Laurie put her teeth together and refused to say any more.

In fact, Leo Rampkin had gone off with Belle Ballantine. Leo was playing his cards right, too. Now was no time to hang around and prejudice Shirley Partridge against himself by playing advocate in the Ballplayer vs. Musician controversy. He would be most unwelcome.

If Keith wanted to be a ballplayer badly enough, and Leo Rampkin was very certain he did, there was nothing Leo could add that would help. It was all up to Keith now and how he really felt.

His sensational performance at Meadowville Diamond, coming on the heels of his Meadowville Fair heroics, had to have turned the trick. If it hadn't, then Leo Rampkin knew nothing about growing minds.

And therefore had no business being a schoolteacher.

Or the personal manager of a big baseball star.

Which he wanted to be.

9

SHIRLEY'S BAD BOY

☐ "Keith, we have to talk."

"I know, Mom."

"It won't be easy, either. Now that I've seen you in action."

"What do you mean, Mom?"

"What do I mean? I mean you really are good. You really can hit and catch a ball. You're a born athlete. So I know you aren't just a boy giving in to a whim. You have a real decision to make, Keith. I'd like to try to help you make it. One way or the other."

The scene was as before. Up in Keith Partridge's bedroom with the lord of the room lying on the bed, fidgeting and staring up at the ceiling. Shirley Partridge had seated herself carefully at his side, looking down at him.

"We have to talk, Keith. Honestly. We've been over this before, I know. But it's different now."

He stirred uncomfortably, avoiding her eyes.

"Why is it different? Just another ball game—"

"It's different. Believe me. Mr. Perkins manages a ball club in the minor leagues. Leo Rampkin invited him down just to see you. He was very impressed with you, Keith. He told me you had a real career ahead of you if you went after it."

Keith swung his eyes down from the ceiling to his mother's face.

"That gray-haired man that was sitting with Leo?"

"Yes."

"Gee. I wondered about him. Didn't talk to him at all. But Leo kind of let me know who he was. I thought he was kidding."

Shirley shook her head, all too ruefully.

"Leo Rampkin doesn't kid about anything. I misjudged him. He wasn't just making conversation last Sunday when we brought him home for dinner. He thinks you should play baseball. And if he has his way, you will. Make no bones about that."

Keith's eyes suddenly shone.

"Wow. They really both think I can do it, huh?"

"They most certainly do. But what do you think?"

Their eyes locked and Keith couldn't take the steadiness of her stare. He shifted away, uncomfortably.

"I . . . just don't know—"

She shook her head, sadly.

"That's no good, Keith. You have to know. You have to make up your mind."

"Gee, Mom." He squirmed visibly. "Give me some time."

"Sure. But will you remember something? We're still the Partridge Family. Musicians A singing act of which you are a member. And we are due at the Twilight Room next week and nobody in this house is doing any rehearsing lately. Least of all you. You're stale by now I'll bet. And you don't seem to care any more about playing the guitar. So I do want to know. Mr. Perkins wants you to play for his club the last month of the season. I have to know one way or the other before I give him an answer. I can't have you suddenly packing up and going off in the middle of the night with stars in your eyes, leaving us all high and dry. Now what is your decision?"

He protested very vehemently, saying he'd never run out on the kids and her but she couldn't quite believe him as much as she wanted to. That feverish glint was still in his eyes and his voice had an uncertain edge to it. Like he was trying to convince himself of something.

"Gosh, Mom, what kind of guy do you think I am—a cop-out? I'd never pull a stunt like that—"

She sighed. "We don't always mean what we say. Or do what we say. How will you feel three weeks from now when you might get this baseball bug again?"

He grinned. His wide-open, infectious smile. Her heart gladdened with love for him. He was quite a boy, no matter what he did.

"I like to play. I am good, I think. Leastways everybody seems to think so. Anyhow—not this year. Heck, I still got to get a little older. And bigger. Maybe next year I'll take Mr. Perkins up on his offer. But—gee, Mom, I couldn't run out on you and the kids, now."

"You're sure, Keith? Very sure?"

"Sure I'm sure."

"But you could be a star. A solo big one. You'd like that. Anybody would. And if you can really be a big-time ball-player, you might be tossing away a great career—fame, money, everything—if you stay with us."

Suddenly, he looked sheepish and not so sure, any more.

"Cut it out," he growled. "I'm a long way from Coopers-town, Mom. You don't get into Baseball's Hall of Fame until after like twenty years of playing top ball."

Her grin matched his and the feeling of relief in her heart was overwhelming. Yet she couldn't quite shake off a feeling of apprehension. She knew she had done most of the talking and like people who do in a two-sided conversation, she re-mained not very sure of all the things she had heard.

"Okay," she said, kissing him lightly on the forehead. "I'll tell Mr. Perkins to come around next year. If the offer is still open. And I hope you don't regret your decision, Keith Par-tridge. It isn't everyone who has a chance to turn down Cooperstown."

He winked at her, smiling.

"See you at the Twilight Room, baby." It was a pretty good imitation of Humphrey Bogart. Shirley Partridge laughed her appreciation. The gloom of the evening evaporated in a flash. When she had come home from the game, getting all the children finally to bed, she had come up to this room with the single purpose of talking to Keith about his plans for the present and the future. He had put up so lit-tle resistance that it was baffling, as well as gladsome. But she couldn't quite shake off the feeling that she hadn't won anything. That all that had been gained was a delay.

Still, it was something.

At least, Keith had reached some kind of decision.

One had to be grateful for small blessings.

Keith yawned. "I'm tired. Guess I'll hit the hay—"

"Me, too. What would you like for breakfast, baseball star?"

"Oh, anything you make is okay with me, Mom."

"Good boy."

With that, she left him, closing the door softly.

Once she was out in the hall, Keith Partridge winced very visibly and held his left hand up to the light of the room. If Shirley Partridge had still been in the room, her frightened wail might have been heard all the way to Pasadena.

The thumb of Keith's left hand was a swollen, bloated object almost a size larger than usual. He had kept his hand out of sight all through the interview and with good reason. The darn thing had started to swell right after the game. And hurt, too. It felt like a million needles were pricking it. Now, hours later, the damage was really done. The thumb hurt like blazes and if anything registered on Keith's brain it was the simple truth of what Shirley Partridge had told him last time in this very room. How does a guitar player play the guitar with a damaged thumb that looked like something out of a Walt Disney cartoon?

The mishap had occurred in the ball game, of course.

In that sensational inning when he had electrified the crowd by running in and shoestringing a sure hit off the grass top with a wonderful catch. But the ball had jammed his thumb before it bounced into his glove hand. The sort of injury most baseball catchers are plagued with. Hard to heal and time-consuming. Some backstops missed a week's worth of games after a bad break like that. And at the moment, Keith's chances of playing guitar in the Twilight Room were very slim indeed.

But the worst part of it was, he still wanted to play baseball. And he still wanted to keep up his obligations to the family. And he knew, instinctively, he couldn't do both.

And how in the world was he going to avoid telling Mom about the thumb?

If she couldn't see it for herself tomorrow.

Keith Partridge turned his face into his bed pillow and groaned aloud, muffling the anguish of the sound.

Some days, it didn't pay a guy to get up out of bed.

This had been one of them.

Shirley Partridge, once she had left Keith's room, had intended to go directly to her own room, determined to get some sleep and put aside, temporarily, the problem of what to do with a growing son. But she had to pass Laurie's bedroom en route. And in so doing, inadvertently stumbled onto yet another problem.

The sound of crying, soft, steady and unmistakable, issued from behind the door. The noise continued in a series of broken snatches of sobs. Shirley paused in consternation.

Normally, she might have pressed on and minded her own business—after all, a young girl's tears can very well be a private affair—but so many strange forces seemed to be working in the Partridge household, she didn't want any more surprises.

Grimly, determinedly, she softly pushed the door in and entered the room. For once, not knocking seemed the correct thing to do.

She was right.

Laurie, huddled on her bed, curled up against a pillow, with her blonde hair trailing, was shuddering with sobs. She didn't even hear her mother come in. Not until Shirley had gone to her and softly put her arms on the quaking shoulders did Laurie stir.

And then it was to sob even more deeply and surrender to the warm embrace of her mother. Shirley's heart filled with love. Laurie hadn't come to her like this in years.

She patted the blonde head at her shoulder with a loving hand.

"Laurie . . . honey . . . ?"

"Oh, Mom!"

It was a heartbroken wail.

"Come on, now . . . slow down . . . want to talk to me about it?"

Laurie shook her head, her tears staining Shirley's housecoat.

"Please, honey. If something is bothering you, tell me. Maybe we can work it out. Huh?"

Laurie pulled away, planting her back against the headboard of the bed. Shirley moved back to give her room. The sobs began to subside. Laurie sniffled into a kerchief she had produced from the folds of her dressing gown. In the darkness of the room, Shirley could see the growing beauty of her daughter; the pure outlines and features of a girl who would one day grow into a true beauty.

For a poignant moment, she wanted to cry herself. But she

held back the tears and assumed a steadfast attitude. After all, she had to help her daughter, not join her in a good cry.

Laurie calmed down and blew lustily into the kerchief.

"It's Leo Rampkin, I suppose," Shirley Partridge murmured sagely.

Laurie's eyes glinted in the dimness and her mouth turned down in a thin, hard line.

"I hate him," she whispered, fiercely.

"Sure you do. But why?"

Laurie shook her head.

"Come on," Shirley urged. "You started to tell me. Don't stop now. I do want to know."

"It's just that—" Laurie started to blurt then a quick sob escaped her only to be gone again. "He had no business acting like that. Not after the way we treated him so nice—"

"Laurie," Shirley said very patiently, "please start at the beginning. And then we'll see how bad it really is. Okay?"

Still upset visibly, Laurie nodded and spanked out at her huddled knees. She didn't look at her mother but began to speak out her troubles. And heartbreaks. And heartaches. They were all of a piece, and as Shirley had expected, all centered on one Leo Rampkin, the gorgeous schoolteacher.

A teenage crush can be a very bad thing for a sensitive girl. And if she was anything, Laurie Partridge was certainly sensitive. Perhaps more so than the average girl.

". . . Mom . . . he invited us to the ball park. I considered myself his date. Nobody else's. I even called up all my friends to tell them that. So what does he do? Belle Ballantine of all people! I told her too and then Leo Rampkin goes and spoils everything by going home with her after the ball game! Right in front of everybody. It was like he dropped me cold! And you know Belle! She'll rub it in until the Year Two Thousand! Oh, Mom. How can I face anybody ever again? All my friends? I'm telling you—Leo Rampkin made me the laughingstock of Meadowville this very night! And I'll never forgive him for that. Not ever!"

More tears poured forth now, accompanied by miserable, self-pitying murmurs of worthlessness and ugly duckling syndrome. Shirley consoled her fair daughter as best she could but she instinctively knew it would be a hopeless job this night. Laurie was going to have her cry and that was that. You can't argue or reason with a girl in the throes of love and suspected humiliation.

"Laurie, listen to me—"

She had to try, anyway. As a mother and a counsellor. What else were mothers for after children are no longer helpless babies?

Laurie sniffled again, drying her eyes.

"I'm listening, Mom. But it's no use. I wish I were dead . . ."

"Well, I'm glad you're not. But it isn't as bad as you think. Why not look on the bright side? I agree with you that Leo Rampkin committed an unfortunate blunder. But maybe he had something very important to discuss with Belle Ballantine. Something that had to do with school. Like her classes. After all, you're just assuming he took a personal interest in her. And you know, that's not allowed, really. He's a teacher. Besides, the same rule applies to you, honey. It's not really fair of you to assume that Leo Rampkin was your date tonight. Remember, he has an interest in your brother. All this baseball business—"

"I don't care," Laurie said hotly. "He likes me. I know he does!"

"Nobody is saying otherwise. But there are all kinds of likes, aren't there? Why jump the gun, honey? Why not wait and see how everything turns out?"

"But it's *so* humiliating!"

"I suppose it is. From your point of view."

"That's the only point of view there is. For me. Can't you see that, Mom?"

"Yes. I can. So what do we do now?"

Laurie suddenly shrugged and almost smiled.

"I'm going to make a voodoo doll of Leo Rampkin and stick pins in it. That's what."

Shirley chuckled.

"That could help. At least it will make you feel better."

"Serve him right, too. The handsome beast."

Shirley sighed, patting her on the knee.

"Think you can get some sleep, now? It *is* very late."

"Uh huh . . ." Laurie yawned. "Are all men beasts, Mom?"

"No comment. Not until tomorrow. Now close your eyes and go to sleep. And no more crying. And that's an order."

"I still hate him. But I'll go to sleep."

"Good girl."

They embraced briefly and then Shirley tiptoed out of the

room. Her head was a riot of mixed emotions. Laurie lay back on the bed and then turned over on her right side the way she had ever since she was a baby. Nostalgia stabbed at Shirley Partridge. But she delayed no longer and exited from the room.

Yet, her mind seethed with unhappiness. Despite the temporary abatements of the problems of Keith and Laurie Partridge, she felt herself somehow losing control of the situations springing up all around her. Things were just getting out of hand.

The Twilight Room engagement was looming closer and closer. Just a mere week away, now.

And yet, she was further and further from real peace of mind on all fronts.

Deeply troubled, she went to bed.

Nothing worked.

Try as she might she could not get to sleep. It was a hopeless situation. The problems of the evening just wouldn't go away. Twin horrors loomed in her unhappy mind. Shirley Partridge, mother and musical singing star, could not sleep because she knew in her mind that the problems of Keith and Laurie Partridge were far from settled.

Something had to be done.

Something concrete and decisive.

But what?

Sleepless and worn out, she had scorned taking an aspirin or a sleeping pill. She had lain awake long after she had left Laurie's room, trying to come up with a satisfactory solution. None came for awhile until the inevitable occurred to her. She hadn't even had to grasp for the answer. It had come to her as all things do—unbidden, unannounced—and yet, all of a sudden, the answer was there. She was actually amazed that she hadn't thought of it much sooner. Of course!

REUBEN KINKAID!

Business manager, father confessor, port in a storm, harried, grim, yet lovable, dependable, reliable Reuben Kinkaid. Surely, Reuben would know what to do. He always did. Emergencies were meat and drink to him, especially when any of his clients were threatened. Nor would the lateness of the hour matter to him. Reuben always wanted to be wanted, and if it was a business problem, so much the better. Hadn't he always impressed on Danny Partridge the exquisite difference between just being a dollars-and-cents agent as opposed to a *personal* business manager? Of course, he had. And more than once—it was one of the many things Shirley Partridge admired him for.

Mind made up now, Shirley sprang from her bed and reached for the pink Princess phone on her bedstand. It was almost twelve o'clock but she couldn't wait until morning and a more decent time. Reuben would understand. Anything that threatened the status quo of the Partridge Family would get top priority with him.

Still, even as she dialed his home telephone number, with trembling fingers, she couldn't help feeling a bit silly and hysterical. Reuben might just pooh-pooh all her fears and foolish fancies. But it was a risk she was prepared to run. Anything was better than carrying the load all by herself.

Anything!

She had to wait for seven rings of the phone before someone picked up the receiver at the other end of the line. Shirley took a deep breath and controlled her beating heart. But she knew it would be a monumental relief to talk about her family problems with somebody else besides the people involved.

". . . ah . . . yah . . . who's this . . . ?"

Dismayed, she recognized his voice, realizing suddenly that she had obviously roused him in the middle of a deep sleep.

"Reuben, I'm so sorry, this is Shirley Partridge. I guess I woke you up, huh?"

There was a pregnant pause in which she was certain she heard him fume. But you could never really tell with Reuben Kinkaid; he was a man who seldom smiled. Not even when business was good.

"You guessed right . . ." Now, she heard his baffled yawn. He had very obviously looked at a clock somewhere. "Say, what are you calling me for at this time? It's almost midnight —" Then, his voice octaved as a note of worry penetrated the fog of his subconscious. "Hey, everything is all right, isn't it?"

"Not exactly, Reuben. That's why I'm calling."

"Shirley, I want to know all there is to know—" He was wide awake now and very unhappy. "Don't spare me. If anything bad has happened to you or the kids—"

He sounded so much like a worried father, she couldn't restrain a flood of genuine affection for him. Good old Reuben. Now she knew she had been wise to call him. She felt fifty percent better already.

She took a deep breath and plunged into her tale of woe.

"Now, slow down, Reuben. Take it easy. It's not as bad as all that, and I didn't call you in the middle of the night to give you a stroke. The kids are all as healthy as carrots and I'm in the pink, too." She sighed. "I wish it was something as simple as a case of measles. You could cure that with a pill or something. No, dear manager, this is a trifle more complex. And it might take a little more time."

She had really thrown him for a loss with that incredible comment. He fairly choked on his end of the line.

"Shirley Partridge, if you don't tell me what's going on down there while my back's turned, I'll disown you. Give, girl, give!"

"Well, Reuben—" She made it as gentle as possible on him. "What do you think of the idea of Keith Partridge playing center field someday for the New York Mets and becoming the biggest baseball star of them all? Not right away, you understand, but soon—like say starting next month?"

He couldn't speak. He made a strangling sound from his end of the phone. So she kept on talking, giving him some time to assimilate the startling news. She could well imagine how ridiculous it all must sound to the man who represented one of the top five musical acts in all the country. The Partridge Family—whom Reuben Kinkaid had guided to the top of the competitive heap. Virtually, all by his lonesome.

". . . and also, just for extra icing, young Laurie Partridge has decided she is in love again. With a schoolteacher named Leo Rampkin. So rehearsing for the Twilight Room is the last thing on her young mind, too. Nice, huh? I just don't know how I'm going to get these kids ready for the biggest night club engagement of their careers. Do you, Reuben?"

Reuben Kinkaid collected some oxyen and got his wits back, again.

"You're putting me on, Shirley?"

"I wish I was, Reuben."

"Baseball? Love? That's kid stuff!"

"Don't knock it unless you've tried it, Reuben. Keith is marvelous as a ballplayer and Leo Rampkin is one of the handsomest young men I have ever seen in twenty years of boywatching."

Reuben Kinkaid groaned.

"This sounds serious. What are we going to do, Shirley?"

She laughed in spite of her bad feelings.

"I called you, remember? The message was—H-E-L-P!"

"All right, all right," he snapped. "I get the message. I'll be there as soon as I can tomorrow. First thing. Meanwhile, I wish you'd give me some of the gory details. About how all this started . . . and so forth . . ."

So Shirley Partridge did.

And Reuben Kinkaid listened.

And in the end, it all sounded even more dire than ever.

Like something that would truly upset the Partridge Family applecart, the one that Reuben Kinkaid had labored so diligently to build.

That Shirley Partridge had loved so fervently to push.

10

QUO VADIS, PARTRIDGE?

☐ Jimmy Perkins and Leo Rampkin met the next morning for a conference, using a breakfast appointment as a good excuse for a strategy review. Perkins, the gray-haired eagle of the minors, was still waiting for some word from Mother Partridge on her decision concerning her talented son. He was due to rejoin his club that evening for an important series of three games which would do much to decide the pennant ambitions of his team but somehow he hadn't wanted to leave town without a definite yes or no from Shirley Partridge. The addition of slugging Keith this late in the race for the flag could make all the difference in the world. Leo Rampkin, just as eager as Perkins, to get going on his own master plan, was beginning to get overly anxious, too. After all, one mother like Shirley Partridge could turn the world around, if she got it into her head to stop Keith from doing what he wanted to do. Keith Partridge, to get right down to the nitty-gritty, was still a minor, was he not?

He certainly was, show business or not!

Perkins and Rampkin had a breakfast of orange juice, scrambled eggs, toast and coffee, in the coffee shop of the hotel where Perkins was staying. The manager, keen-eyed as ever, looked slightly disgruntled that sunny morning and Leo Rampkin was quick to spot the fact that things had to move a little faster or Perkins would be clearing out of town without Keith Partridge nailed down to a contract or some kind of agreement. There is just so much time a baseball man can spend in the pursuit of new talent. Rampkin knew that you always had to strike while the iron was hot.

"Don't worry, Jimmy. Shirley Partridge is bound to call you sometime this morning. I'm sure of it."

"She'd better, Leo. Time's awasting. My train pulls out at two P.M. sharp and I can't hang around a minute longer than that. We play Sand Rock tonight and it's a big series and I have to be there."

"Maybe you could call her—"

Perkins laughed sourly, shaking his head as he sipped his coffee.

"You may be a hot-shot teacher, Leo, but anybody could tell you're no horse trader. If I called her now it would put me in a bad bargaining position. I'd sound desperate no matter how smoothly I made my pitch. No, Leo. I have to stand pat until the lady calls me. That's the way the ball bounces."

"I guess you know what you're talking about."

"I do, believe me. Our greatest asset right now is the kid himself. If Keith Partridge really wants to play baseball, the odds are pretty good he's been after his mother since last night, begging her to let him go. I just hope the boy is as good a salesman as he is a natural athlete."

Leo Rampkin nodded.

"Mrs. Partridge is a nice lady. Intelligent, too. She's not the typical show business mother. If Keith really wants to cut loose from her, she won't stand in his way. Just you wait and see."

"I am waiting," Perkins agreed sourly, "and I hope to heck you know what you're talking about. You don't know how much I need a right-hand hitting outfielder who can hit with men on base and catch anything that's hit in his direction."

"I know," Leo Rampkin said vehemently. "That's why I called you in the first place. Remember?"

Jimmy Perkins stared at him over the rim of his coffee cup. The keen eyes were openly curious.

"I've been thinking about that, Leo. I mean, what's in this for you? Just want to see a young kid make the grade, love of baseball, or what? You must have other things to keep you busy. Or is there more here than meets the eye? You always were one step ahead of everybody else, Leo. You're smart.

Sometimes too smart for your own good. So what is it *really* this time?"

Leo Rampkin laughed. A trifle harshly but not too unkindly. He looked at the older man with a shade of genuine affection and more than a little added respect. He realized all too suddenly that he had not fooled Jimmy Perkins.

"Well, Jimmy, to tell you the truth, I have been kind of feathering my own nest. You see, this being a schoolteacher isn't exactly all it's cracked up to be. Fact is, I don't make enough money. And I don't think I ever will. So I see a very strong chance in Keith Partridge helping me write my own ticket out of this hick town. If Shirley Partridge lets him go, I intend to become the boy's personal manager. From the bottom up. That is, if you have no objections."

Jimmy Perkins whistled under his breath and reached for another dab of buttered toast. He grinned from ear to ear, marveling at the younger man across the table.

"Everybody needs a manager or an agent of some kind, Leo. You deliver Keith Partridge to me or my club and you can make your own deal. If it's okay with the boy and his mother, it's no skin off my nose. But—"

Before he could go on, a waitress materialized at the table, asking his name and then telling him there was a phone call for him in the lobby. Leo flung him a quick look as he got up to leave the table. Perkins was smiling a grim smile. Leo felt his mouth go dry. Jimmy Perkins looked down at him and grunted, "That's probably Mrs. Partridge now. I guess we'll have our answer soon enough. I hope for both our sakes, it's the right answer, Leo."

Rampkin blurted, "It's got to be yes. She couldn't stand in his way. She shouldn't! Not when a boy is a natural talent like Keith is—"

"Steady, son. It's a free country. And don't push the panic button just yet. We still don't know what she decided. If it's strike three—" Jimmy Perkins shrugged, smiled again, turned on his heel, and stalked out to the lobby. Leo Rampkin watched him go, suddenly feeling a deep sense of foreboding in the pit of his stomach. He abruptly realized just how much he was depending on riding the shoulders of Keith Partridge out of Meadowville. To the stars. To fame and fortune.

Shirley Partridge had to say yes.

She had to let Keith go. Had to let him do his own thing.

She just had to do the *right* thing.

95

Or there was no justice left in the whole wide world.

Leo Rampkin broke into a cold sweat of expectancy waiting for Jimmy Perkins to come back from the lobby.

One telephone call for Leo Rampkin had suddenly assumed all the characteristics of a Life or Death pronouncement.

He had never understood before what it was like to be uncertain about one's future. For once in his life, he didn't have a satisfactory answer for Failure, if it came. Failure was a comparative stranger.

Leo Rampkin had known nothing but Success in his time. Waterloo was not for the likes of him.

That was for Napoleon and other assorted losers.

He had a second cup of coffee as he fidgeted, waiting for Jimmy Perkins.

Jimmy Perkins was philosophic. Baseball managers have to be. In a game that can be won or lost by inches, where the foul line calls a ball fair or foul and costs victory and pins defeat, he was very used to the ups-and-downs of Fate. So Shirley Partridge's important decision came to him over the telephone wire without the horror and tragedy it would have impinged on Leo Rampkin's ears.

"I'm sorry, Mr. Perkins. But we've decided. Keith and I both, that is. He wants to stay with the Partridge Family and I can't say that I'm not glad. He's a fine musician and we do need him."

"I'm sorry too, Mrs. Partridge. For different reasons, of course."

"I know what you mean. And I know how you feel. You really think Keith could amount to something in a baseball uniform and I'm sure you know what you're talking about. I appreciate that, Mr. Perkins. Just as I appreciate the manner in which you went about this. Not going behind my back or trying to influence Keith in any way. You're a gentleman, Mr. Perkins."

He laughed ruefully at that.

"And you're a lady. And there are several umpires in my league who'd give you some argument about my manners."

"Just the same. I mean it. And you know—Keith can still go out for baseball next season, if he still has a mind to. I wouldn't stand in his way. And if he keeps on growing the way he has been, I'm not so sure I'd be able to stop him, either, if he made up his mind to break out on his own."

Jimmy Perkins laughed warmly.

"The Partridge Family, huh? Guess I'll have to buy some records now and hear what a potentially great ballplayer sounds like on the guitar."

"He's fine," Shirley Partridge laughed, too. "A real musician. I think you'd be as proud of him as I am."

"I'm proud of him already."

There was no more to be said. Both sensed that so Jimmy Perkins made the break first. With genuine regret.

"Well, goodbye, Mrs. Partridge. And all the luck in the world in the future. And I mean that. From the bottom of the bat rack, lady."

"Goodbye, Mr. Perkins. Thanks for being so understanding."

When she hung up, Shirley Partridge experienced a mixed feeling of relief and annoyance. Relief that Jimmy Perkins had been a good loser and annoyance that she had already put in an SOS to Reuben Kinkaid. It hardly seemed necessary, now. Keith had resigned himself to do the right thing, Perkins was leaving the scene, and now the Partridge Family could get back to normal. Barring Laurie's heartbreak with Leo Rampkin. Still, she couldn't quite lose a feeling of uneasiness.

Sighing, she told herself that the whole family better knuckle down to rehearsals for the Twilight Room engagement.

Or else!

When Jimmy Perkins hung up and eased out of the lobby booth and returned to the coffee shop, he felt nothing but a deep regret. Keith Partridge had shown him fantastic things the night before. Ranging all over the outfield, hitting every kind of pitch thrown to him, making all the impossible plays. It would have been a marvelous experience watching that kind of talent grow into something special but—if the kid wanted to be a music maker instead of a ballplayer, there was no use bucking it. He was sure that Shirley Partridge had not been an unfair influence. She had seemed as fair and square as she looked and sounded. Chances are the kid himself just didn't love the game as much as he ought to with the kind of talent he had.

Still, it was a crying shame.

As far as Jimmy Perkins was concerned, the world needed a lot more DiMaggios than it needed Elvis Presleys. Or whatever it was the kid really did.

Leo Rampkin's face fell all the way to the floor when Perkins told him what Shirley Partridge had said. Jimmy Perkins was amazed. He hadn't fully appreciated until that very moment exactly how much Leo had been counting on a Yes answer. The blood drained right out of Leo's handsome face and he looked as if he was going to be sick.

"She can't—" Leo Rampkin spluttered. "She just can't—"

"Well, she did," Jimmy Perkins grunted, reaching for the check, "and she's in her rights and there's nothing me or you or anybody else can do about it. So make up your mind, Leo. It's strike three and we're both out."

Leo Rampkin shook his head, like a dumb dog, unable to comprehend.

"No—it isn't fair. That woman doesn't know what she's doing. She's ruining a great career! A career that could outshine everybody."

Jimmy Perkins smiled slowly.

"Hold on, now. Keith Partridge is good but there's a lot he'd have to prove yet. Over a lot of seasons. Don't lose your perspective altogether, Leo. Rome wasn't built in a day. Neither is a major league ballplayer."

Leo Rampkin wasn't listening. His eyes were glittering strangely and his voice was low and hurried, as if he had just thought of something and the sooner he attended to it, the better. Joining Jimmy Perkins as he strode out of the coffee shop toward the lobby, Leo controlled himself.

"I know you have to get back, Jimmy, but don't give up on the kid just yet. I think I can still deliver him. I've got an idea."

"Suit yourself, Leo. But don't knock yourself out on my account. And see that you don't do anything foolish, either. The Partridges are nice people. Don't make any waves. Can't you be a good loser?"

At that, Leo Rampkin faced him squarely in the lobby where potted palms, tiled floor and soft chairs made up the decor.

"You were never a good loser, Jimmy Perkins. Why should I be?"

Perkins chuckled. "You got me there, son. But fight square, whatever you do. If you can still talk the boy into joining the club, okay. But I don't want any kickbacks from Mrs. Partridge. It has to be what everybody wants all around. In the end. Got me?"

"Got you. Leave it to me . . ." Leo Rampkin shook his head. "I just can't let her make him throw away a great career just out of family loyalty. I know he wants to play baseball. You know it, too. How could he play as well as he does if he wasn't just busting to be a ballplayer?"

"Yeah," Jimmy Perkins admitted, in spite of his conversation with Shirley Partridge only minutes earlier, "you got me there too, Leo. I wondered about that, too. He sure goes after it like he loves it. You can always tell. Lot of Willie Mays in the way that boy played last night."

"Then it's settled," Leo said with more jubilance than he had shown. "It's only ten o'clock. I still have four hours until you catch that train. You give me four hours—and I bet you I'll be back with Keith Partridge. I can do a lot in four hours."

Jimmy Perkins shrugged.

"It's your ball game. I'll be here when you want me. Till two. Good luck, Leo. Though personally, I don't think you've got a chance. Ma Partridge is no dope. Neither is Keith from what I've seen of him. But go get 'em, tiger. And I'll root for you just the same."

Leo Rampkin wrung the manager's hand warmly. His eyes had lit up again.

"Just wait and see, Jimmy. Wait and see."

Perkins chuckled wryly.

"What else have I got to do that's better?"

In Partridge House, Danny Partridge was doing a crossword puzzle in the living room. His red head was lowered intently over the problem, pencil poised, eyes screwed up in concentration. Shirley Partridge came in from the kitchen, the last of the breakfast dishes done. She frowned at her son and patted his head as she passed behind his chair.

"Stop scowling, Danny. You'll put more wrinkles in your forehead."

"Mom."

"Yes, honey?"

"What's a three letter word meaning *trouble?*"

"Trouble in three letters? Let me see . . ."

"It's not *fix* or any word like that. I tried that already."

Shirley Partridge sighed.

"How about *woe?* W-O-E. That sounds like it might do it."

"Hmmmm." Danny Partridge considered the three empty spaces and the areas crossing it. "*Woe.* Yeah, Mom. *Woe* is good. Thanks."

Shirley Partridge smiled ruefully.

Woe is good. . . .

Out of the mouths of babes!

11

KINKAID, KINKAID

□ Shirley Partridge, all her mental troubles carefully set aside, gathered the family in the living room. It was high time she and the kids got down to brass tacks. Brass tacks like rehearsals and preparing for the sort of thing everybody did best. Namely the playing and singing of music.

As she gathered her little army of domestic talent, she was cutely aware of something strange and alien in the atmosphere of the room. Of course, Simone was lying quietly in one corner, her canine tongue licking assiduously at her snout while she watched the kids prepare to go into their act but it was something more than that. There was a general aura of lassitude and so-what? apparent in the attitudes of all the children.

Even as she gathered up the sheet music and passed it around the room, the remarkable lack of enthusiasm from all hands was deplorable. True it was Tuesday morning and no real cause for celebration but with the Twilight Room playing date looming at the end of the week, it was strangely disquieting to see the kids so gloomy and down in the dumps. Shirley tried to fathom the situation without giving voice to her fears.

So she surveyed and studied the kids as they glumly accepted the sheet music and propped it up on their individual stands. They were also very lazily fingering their instruments. There was no joy or gladness in the act itself. Which was really unique. The kids, whatever their present troubles might be, had always found a great release in playing their instruments and singing their songs.

Shirley Partridge quietly watched her children.

It sure was a funereal-looking group, for one so young!

Keith Partridge was idly plucking at his electric guitar with his right hand. His left one was dangling disinterestedly at his side. There was no expression on his face at all as he scanned the music his mother had handed him. Of course, Shirley realized that Keith might still be mentally locked up in the great sacrifice he had willingly made for the good of the family. Namely, giving up a possibly great career as the new DiMaggio to stay with the Partridges and earn his coffee and cake (and Fame) as an integral part of a family act. That could be understood . . . Keith's disinterest this morning.

And Laurie Partridge!

Shirley had never seen her so dowdy. For one thing, she had hardly brushed her long brownish-blonde hair and the ribbon she had intertwined in the tresses was a poorly constructed thing. Laurie's face was pale and wan, too. As if she had cried all night. And as she sat on her high stool with her hands folded in her lap, staring blankly ahead, since her function with the group was purely as a singer, Shirley well knew what was troubling her lovely daughter. The Leo Rampkin romance, which had received a severe setback in the person of Belle Ballantine, was dying miserably. Slowly and miserably. Shirley's heart went out to her offspring but what could she really do for her except sympathize, empathize, and hope that Time, the Great Healer, would work his magic. But for now, the teenage hurt and shame must be enormous.

Yes, she could understand the reactions of Keith and Laurie but what excuse was there for Danny and Christopher and Tracy? Their behavior this morning was outlandish.

And unexpected.

Red-haired Danny was poised over his guitar, absent-mindedly plucking with both thumbs something that sounded like a dirgelike version of *Chopsticks*. Danny, who usually always smiled, wore no smile today. Indeed, his freckles stood out starkly because he was not laughing. Which was surprising, too. Danny was usually the spark and goad of all Partridge Family rehearsals.

Baffled, Shirley swung her attention to Christopher and little Tracy, the youngest. There again was more mystery and more wonder. Something else to ponder over and conjure with.

Christopher was lying with his head on his drums, arms folded into a makeshift pillow beneath his head, as if he hadn't gotten the necessary amount of sleep the night before. Which was ridiculous because Shirley herself had tucked him in no later than ten o'clock before she had had her quiet talks with Keith and Laurie. But the signs were unmistakable. Christopher was yawning loudly, and at very frequent intervals.

Little Tracy, whose main contribution to the Partridge Family act was a tambourine and a sweet singing voice was staring down at her hands as if she was trying to read them. Which was not exactly usual behavior either for a young lady of her tender years. Her amazement growing apace with each passing second, Shirley shook her head and reached for the baton on the music stand at her elbow. She tapped with the thin stick of wood so peremptorily and commandingly that Simone raised her furry head from the floor and growled.

But the kids all responded with less alacrity.

Shirley stood in the center of the room, placed one hand on her left hip and stared at her children. She managed a tight smile but somewhere inside her maternal bosom danger signals began to unfurl. Something was in the wind, she knew, and being the mother she knew she was going to be the last to know.

Wasn't that how it always was?

But she was also wise enough to start things off with some humor. The light touch, bless it, was usually a good way to get the ball rolling. Especially at rehearsal time.

"All right," she managed with brisk brightness, which she didn't exactly feel, "coming to you direct from Meadowville Cemetery, for an exclusive one night only performance, the singing Partridge Family in all their musical glory. Ah-one, ah-two, ah-three . . ."

The Lawrence Welk imitation, complete with the tap, tap, tap of her slippered toe, usually got laughs all around. And results. But it didn't this time. Nobody smiled or stirred. What was worse, nobody picked up the tempo or their instruments and went into the jump rendition of *Eyes For You I Have* which she had planned as the first number to be rehearsed that morning.

There was a serious silence as Shirley's voice trailed off.

She frowned and stared at the kids.

Briskly, she tapped the baton again on the music stand.

Again, Simone emitted a low growl.

Again, nobody moved.

Shirley Partridge sighed, put down the baton, placed both fingers to her curved mouth and let out a blasting, piercing whistle. The kind men employ to halt fast-moving cabs and truckdrivers use to greet each other on the highway. The sound shattered the stillness of the living room and Simone raced yipping under the long, low sofa to one side of the room. It was laughable the reaction the whistle got.

Keith jumped with a guilty start, Laurie emitted a low shriek, Danny's fingers stuck in his guitar, Christopher snapped erect so fast he nearly sprained his neck and little Tracy jumped to a standing position. Shirley Partridge, unable to restrain herself, laughed happily. Now they all looked normal again. Her children, paying attention to her, instead of being off somewhere in worlds of their own making. And Christopher, as startled as he had been, yawned again.

Keith's face darkened with a show of anger.

"For Pete's sake, Mom, what did you want to do that for?"

"Yeah," Danny said challengingly, "I felt that all the way down to my shoes—"

"And you were meant to," Shirley snapped, losing her smile. "What is this? A wake? We're supposed to be rehearsing and you all sit there moping? What's wrong? If there is something I should know, please tell me so we can get on with the rehearsal. We got a big one coming up and we're all stale and rusty I can tell you."

Little Tracy sat down again and put her knees together.

"Well, I'm ready. I come in on the second bridge and—"

Christopher poked her. "The first, dummy. After Danny and Keith play a chorus. Can't you remember anything at all?"

Laurie flung her head back and stared straight ahead.

"Sorry, Mom. I'm ready now."

Shirley stared directly into Keith Partridge's eyes.

"And you, Keith?"

Suddenly, everyone had turned to look at Keith Partridge. Including all the children. And with a sinking feeling she couldn't have pinned down for the life of her, Shirley knew that the trouble, the aura of something, was centered around Keith. Something all the kids *knew* and she *didn't*. Something she had missed. Someplace, somewhere.

And somehow it made her feel terrible.

"Keith—?" she prodded him, gently.

His head came up. She saw his eyes. Never had she seen them so miserable. His mouth was a thin line of hurt. And his shoulders were in a downcast slump. And his right arm was hitched upward. As if—

His mouth worked.

"Mom, I—"

"Yes?"

"You have to understand. I didn't do it on purpose—"

"Keith." She shook her head. "If you've had any second thoughts about taking Mr. Perkins up on his offer, don't be afraid to tell me. I'm your mother. Haven't I taught you that you must never be afraid to talk to me about anything?"

"Yes, but . . . it's not that . . . but . . ."

She sighed and shook her head slowly. A tear began to edge itself out of the corner of one eye.

"Keith Partridge, will you please tell me what's bothering you? I'm no mind reader although with you kids sometimes I wish I was . . ."

That did it.

She could never have guessed what was ailing him though she would have found out for herself soon enough. Nor could Keith ever have brought himself to put it into words. All the other kids had noticed what was wrong with him at the breakfast table. Shirley Partridge had not. Sometimes mothers are too busy even for such obvious things as injuries to fingers that are needed for the playing of musical instruments.

All the kids' eyes shifted from Keith Partridge to their mother as the oldest member of the family held up his left hand in mute and helpless explanation. And utter abject misery.

The thumb, for all its enormous swelling and balloonlike travesty of human flesh, or perhaps because of it, looked like some make-believe digit. The kind of comic device used by silent film comics and music hall comedians in some ridiculous pantomime.

Shirley Partridge's first reaction was one of sheer disbelief and horror.

She put her hands to her mouth and screamed.

A low, muted, terrible moan that was the culmination of all the frustrations and fears of the past few days.

"*Oh, no, Keith!*" she wailed. "*You didn't!*"

But he had, very obviously.

And from the looks of the damaged thumb, which had known no medical care and nothing more than bathing surreptitiously in hot water and Epsom salts while the rest of the family was asleep, young Keith Partridge was going to have to skip the Twilight Room altogether.

If he could ever play a musical instrument again—

Much less pick up a baseball bat.

Reuben Kinkaid, tie carefully knotted, tropical worsted suit neatly pressed, long blonde hair deftly curling over his worried forehead, arrived in Meadowville that afternoon via the quickest airplane flight he could find. A taxicab service had driven him from the airport to town, which was a good twenty miles' distance. Reuben, his mind beset with Shirley Partridge's telephoned problems, had pushed all solutions to one side. Experience had taught Kinkaid to visit the scene of the problem, survey all the angles, and then formulate his plans for relieving that problem. After all, for all her acumen and level-headedness, Shirley was a woman. And women have the unfortunate habit of making problems bigger than they really are because of their largely emotional make-up. Thus, Reuben Kinkaid easily was troubled but not genuinely alarmed. All he had to do (as far as he was concerned) was talk things over with Keith Partridge, mutter some fatherly advice to Laurie and generally smooth things over. Then would his biggest client, the Partridge Family, be ready to go out and capture the Twilight Room and its audiences, fulfill that exclusive recording contract which he had won from the Emko people and all would be right again.

Kinkaid, as you see, was a militant optimist, despite a hard-headed business tendency to see things as they truly are rather than as he hoped them to be. A quality of personality he was convinced that one day little Danny Partridge would also own.

Great boy, Danny, even if a bit too hard to take because of the amazing shrewdness not usually found in one so young. A ten-year-old financial wizard. Real managerial timbre, that boy!

Meadowville was very hot that day. A ninety-five degree temperature punishing the quiet, sylvan streets of the town and as Kinkaid's cab crawled sluggishly through the baking environs, he clung to his ever-ready attache case, conscious of the sticky feel of the black leather in his fingers. Reuben's tie began to wilt, his worsted suit to crumple. His blonde hair clung damply to his forehead. So he arrived at the Partridge Family domicile in a worse frame of mind than when he had approached it. Sultry weather and uncomfortable cabs are not conducive to a genial personality.

Even a Mark Twain or a Will Rogers would have been irritable under such conditions. Being neither, Reuben Kinkaid was a frayed bundle of nerves when his stalking feet led him up the asphalt driveway of the rambling two-story home where the Partridges hung up their guitars and ambitions. Added to which, he literally barged right into Leo Rampkin standing impatiently on the front stoop awaiting an answer to his repeated knockings on the oaken door.

Handsome Leo, his own ambitions still driving him relentlessly, had appeared on the scene in that precise moment when Keith Partridge had exposed his damaged thumb to his shocked mother's eyes. Hence, the delay in anyone answering the door. Inside the house was transpiring a scene that would have outdone the last act of *Room Service*. Shirley Partridge was having a motherly fit.

And the uproar of cries, explanations and childish excitement seemed to make the house rock on its foundations. Simone was barking furiously.

"Sorry," Leo snapped at Reuben Kinkaid, mistaking his appearance as well as the attache case. "No salesmen today. They're busy."

"Excellent!" Reuben Kinkaid roared, his temper past the breaking or reasoning point. "Do you mind getting out of the way? I'm Reuben Kinkaid. I manage the Partridge Family."

Leo Rampkin's face fell immediately.

Another stumbling block loomed in the roadway of his master plan. He hastened to make apologies.

"Oh, sorry . . . excuse me. I'm Leo Rampkin. I'm Keith's teacher. Did you know that boy could be one of the greatest baseball players that ever swung a bat—?"

"Do tell?" Kinkaid snarled acidly, brushing past him and poking the enamelled door buzzer with pointed emphasis.

"Sure—" Leo continued. "And he could make one hundred thousand dollars a year and—"

"Please, Mr. Rampkin," Reuben Kinkaid said sternly, adjusting his wilted tie and clinging to his attache case with grim purposefulness. "Step aside or I'm going to spit right in your eye."

Leo Rampkin stepped aside.

Justified, Reuben Kinkaid rang the buzzer once more.

Behind the closed door, the pandemonium stilled and running footsteps raced to answer the bell.

12

PARTRIDGE STEW

☐ Jimmy Perkins sat around in his hotel room. He had three courses of action, following a multitude of phone calls he had made that morning once he had left Leo Rampkin and returned to his room. He could either take a nap, watch the clock or read a book. He chose to do none of those things. Instead, he relentlessly took to pacing his room back and forth. While he waited for young Leo Rampkin to pull a rabbit out of his academic hat. A rabbit by the name of Keith Partridge, whom Perkins had to admit to himself looked exactly like the finest ballplaying prospect he had seen since Mickey Mantle came up in the New York Yankees farm system.

There was no question about it in Jimmy Perkins' mind. The Partridge boy had all the tools—the only question was would he give up his career with his mother and brothers and sisters to go along with the national pastime? Perkins wished fervently that Keith would. His most immediate need was a slugging outfielder for his own club, to help them win the flag in their league. As he had conveyed to Leo Rampkin. But beyond that need was the old ballplayer's dream to give a child marvel to the major leagues. A prodigy. So that someday the sports world would point to superstar Keith Partridge and say: *"See him? That's Jimmy Perkins' discovery!"*

Which is why Jimmy Perkins was hanging around Meadowville for the two o'clock train instead of hurrying back to rejoin his team in a bigger hurry than he was showing.

Though his motives were different, Jimmy Perkins shared with Leo Rampkin the big fine dream that Keith Partridge had it in him to turn a baseball league upside down with his exploits.

So he stalked back and forth like a caged tiger.

Or, more specifically, a worried manager.

In another part of town, Belle Ballantine, the fly in Laurie Partridge's ointment, was readying herself to go out and foray into the streets. Belle, her raven-black hair in a sheen of an upsweep, her lithe figure encased in one of her tightest dark dresses, was aglow with warpaint and an inner desire to wrest Leo Rampkin from Laurie's safekeeping. Belle had already won an important battle. The night before, at the ball game, she had gotten Leo Rampkin to escort her home in his own car, thereby throwing mud in Laurie's jealous eye. But now Belle wanted to win the war. She had already mapped out her campaign. That morning she had been busy on the phone in her own chartreuse-walled bedroom, calling every girl that she and Laurie both knew, making darn sure that everyone knew how she had vamped Leo away from Laurie. Then she had learned from Leo's mother how he had gone to the Partridge house to talk to Keith about his career. So Belle, dressed to the nines, and ready to make another killing, right in the heart of enemy territory, was determined to call on the Partridges and score another victory.

There are girls like Belle Ballantine all over the country.

Just as there are girls like Laurie Partridge.

And ever the twain shall meet.

In love and war.

Sooner or later.

So it was that about high noon that day in Meadowville, as Leo Rampkin and Reuben Kinkaid met head-on at the threshold of the Partridge roost on the outskirts of peaceful Meadowville, two other participants in the family drama got restless and made their next move, too. Two completely unrelated individuals, moving from a well-spring of motives that was entirely dissimilar.

Belle Ballantine, driving her zippy little sports car which her indulgent banker-father had given her on her eighteenth

110

birthday, zoomed on toward the Partridge home at better than fifty miles an hour. She was humming happily, sure of victory.

And why not?

Belles of the ball and *femme fatales* are always pretty sure of getting any man they go after.

T'was ever thus, as the poets say.

And Jimmy Perkins, fretting and weary of no news and now very anxious to make a personal last attempt to win over Mother Partridge to the joys and benefits of the major league way of life, hailed a yellow cab outside his hotel and hurriedly entered. Perkins had two hours in which to try and try again. Then he had to catch his train and say goodbye to Keith Partridge forever. And to a dream, too.

But the veteran ballplayer-manager was ready to die fighting. Heck—the woman shouldn't stand in the way if the boy really was so darn good! He, Jimmy Perkins, would never have forgiven himself if he had cleared out of Meadowville without at least one more good old college try. No matter what Leo Rampkin was up to, whatever *that* was, Perkins was convinced that it was up to himself to take a last lick at Shirley Partridge's objections.

Darn the woman, anyhow!

What did dames know about baseball, anyway?

So Jimmy Perkins' cab and Belle Ballantine's sports car bore down on the Partridge house from separate directions but almost at the same time. And in the process they were going to add a lot more confusion to a situation that was rapidly snowballing into a summit conference. As far as the fate of the Partridges was concerned.

And all because a boy named Keith Partridge could swing a bat with the best of them.

Sometimes, blessings come surrounded with misfortunes.

Reuben Kinkaid glared across the living room floor at Leo Rampkin, studiously avoided Danny Partridge's knowing scrutiny and tried not to indulge in a wave of self-pity. Such as why-do-these-things-always-happen-to-me? and why-do-the-Partridges-have-to-be-such-a-talented-bunch-of-trouble-makers? It wasn't easy to control his mixed emotions of rage, frustration and despair. As soon as he had rushed into the house to be greeted by the twin spectacles of Shirley Partridge in motherly tears and Keith Partridge's ridiculously outsized thumb, he had come very close to blowing his cool altogether. But some minor things had saved him. Little Tracy had run to him, her face alive with affection, as she hugged him around the knees, and Christopher had thumped his drums in a rhythmic hello and even Laurie had favored him with a wide-open smile even though her sad eyes told him how miserable she was feeling. Shirley had gone to him, laying her head on his shoulder in mute relief that he had finally turned up and then the topper was Danny Partridge, stalking forward formally, hand out-thrust, exclaiming in firm, no-nonsense tones: "Glad you came, Mister Kinkaid. You're needed here. Maybe now we can straighten this whole mess out!"

Kinkaid's stern resolve to bawl them all out had melted in a flash so he held back, deciding to reserve all his venom for the smart-alecky, slick-looking young college professor he had met at the door. He had wanted to shake Leo Rampkin out of the room and his hair but Shirley Partridge, her tears dried, had insisted that Rampkin stay. Faced with that, Reuben Kinkaid had abandoned an *attitude* altogether and faced Keith Partridge with a mixture of solicitude and reproof.

All the kids clamored to be heard except Keith, who was rather forlornly regarding his guitar and his damaged thumb with alternating expressions of fatalism and sorrow. As much as he didn't want to, Reuben Kinkaid was compelled to place the blame exactly where it belonged. On Keith's doorstep.

"You young idiot," he said, but with soft censure. "How are you going to play the Twilight Room with that hand now? The biggest playing date you folks have ever had and you, the anchor man, with a thumb out of a cartoon!"

Keith nodded unhappily.

"I'm sorry, Mister Kinkaid. But you see the game was—" He shrugged. "I had an idea I might make a good ball-player."

Reuben bridled at that.

"Maybe you could, maybe you can't. But you *are* one of the best teenage guitar players and singers in this world. Why didn't you settle for that?"

Danny spoke up, taking his brother's side, loyally.

"He was really great, Mister Kinkaid. Like eight hits in two games, all kinds of sensational catches and maybe ten runs batted in. You could do better?"

"No," Kinkaid said tartly, his old relationship with Danny reasserting itself, after an all-too-temporary truce. "I'm not paid to make like Johnny Bench. I'm paid to be your business manager. Just like Keith is paid to be a member of the Partridge Family. He shouldn't have risked it all just for couple of ball games."

"Hold on," Leo Rampkin interrupted, coming forward in an aggressive mood. "I have a baseball manager in town that says that Keith could be a one hundred thousand dollar a year ballplayer if he took it up as a career. What do you think of that?"

"I think, Mr. Rampkin," Kinkaid said icily, "that you ought to beat it. Shirley, why is this moonlighter here anyway? What is he—a schoolteacher or a baseball talent scout?"

Before Rampkin could growl a reply or the children take sides, Shirley Partridge laid a restraining hand on Reuben Kinkaid's arm, which had risen in an attitude of self-righteous anger.

"Reuben, I want Leo here. You see—" She paused to look very tenderly at Keith Partridge with a mother's love in her eyes. It shone out of her face. "We all love Keith. Naturally. We all saw him play. He really is great, Reuben. He probably could be another DiMaggio. So I asked him to make a choice. He made it. He chose to stay with the family and do his job. That was a wonderful sacrifice for a boy to make, Reuben. But now this thumb business has come along—and I've had a chance to think a lot about what Keith is giving up. I talked to Mr. Perkins, Leo's manager friend. I said No—and let Keith say No. But I'm not sure any more. Maybe we were both wrong. Keith and I. Maybe he ought to try and go out to be a great ballplayer instead of just another musical Partridge?"

Reuben Kinkaid blinked. Astounded.

"Have you all gone mad? The Twilight Room, remember? And Emko Recording! An exclusive contract. Do I have to remind you that all of you are already stars? That Keith at the tender age of seventeen is already a teenage idol, that half the kids in the country wish they were in his shoes? And you think he ought to give all that up just because he *might* be another DiMaggio or Mickey Mantle? Please, get me a glass of water, somebody—I may faint."

All the Partridges—Shirley, Danny, Christopher, Tracy, Laurie, and even Keith himself—exchanged surprised, almost

113

sheepish looks of dawing awareness. Reuben Kinkaid had spoken nothing but the nice truth. It was one thing to imagine you are celebrated and famous, it is quite another to hear a man you respect and admire and even like say it in so many words. *Of course*, the Partridge Family was famous, and getting more famous all the time.

"Well—" Shirley Partridge began slowly. "That is true—"

"Yeah," Danny chimed in. "We are stars, aren't we?"

"And Keith is big with all the girls," Laurie agreed. "Why, every girl in this town has his picture on her wall and I suppose all the other girls in all the other towns do, too—"

"He's my loving swell brother," Tracy piped up.

"Awwww—" Keith mumbled. "Cut it out. All of you."

"Well, you are," Christopher poked a drumstick at him. "Didn't you get voted America's Favorite Teenager just last year? Sure, you did! You can't do better than that being a ballplayer, I betcha!"

Laurie Partridge, despite her broken heart, smiled at her big brother. She even managed a happy wink.

"You see, Keith? You're very *relevant*, whether you play baseball or not!"

Shirley Partridge waved everybody down and looked at her oldest son. Her eyes softened again. The decision was still with him.

"However you say it, just the same, I want Keith to think about it and make up his own mind. Will you, Keith?"

Leo Rampkin, seeing he was fast losing ground along with his big plan to maneuver himself out of schoolteaching into an impresario's gaudy career, began to fight back. He ignored Reuben Kinkaid's glare and jostled past him to put his arguments to Keith directly. Keith, who was still ruefully regarding the catastrophe his thumb had become. The finger was bloated and empurpled beyond belief.

"Keith, you're a star all right. But you could be a bigger star with baseball. You could endorse sporting goods, go on tours, make movies—why books would be written about you—"

Reuben Kinkaid growled in his throat and took a step forward, taking Leo Rampkin by the elbow. He spun him around. Both men were at eye level and glaring now, looking ready to lock horns.

"Look, son," Kinkaid said in a flat, dead voice, "I've had enough of this. Why don't you butt out? You have no interest in this family beyond a self-motivated one. You dig me? I haven't slugged a guy since World War Two and he was a nasty top sergeant who made me peel too many potatoes but believe me, boy, you're getting me pretty close to the mark. So scram now while the scramming is good, huh?"

Leo Rampkin, feeling he was fighting a losing battle, teetered back on his toes. His two hands came up in a boxing pose. His normally handsome face now wore a grimace that made him look considerably less handsome. And much less learned.

"*Leo!*" Laurie Partridge cried, amazed at the sudden change in him. "Don't you dare hit Mister Kinkaid!"

"Yeah," Danny added his two cents worth. "Don't you dare!"

Reuben Kinkaid blinked again, his face getting redder by the second. He matched Leo Rampkin's stance and circled warily, fists poised. Shirley Partridge stepped between them and restored order as Keith tried to scramble from his stool, almost banging his injured thumb in the process. Simone the dog started barking all over again.

"Now, stop it, you two," Shirley blurted. "That won't solve anything—"

"Oh, no?" Reuben challenged her. "It would make me feel just marvelous—" He had lost his businesslike mien altogether. Leo Rampkin, knowing he had somehow lost his chance at the brass ring, was now furious, too, and spoiling for a fight. Any kind of a fight. He just didn't seem to care any more what happened. Shirley cried out.

"Reuben, behave yourself. Leo, you're a guest in my house and I order you to stop. Both of you. Isn't it bad enough that we have to reach some kind of decision without all this fuss? Look, you're frightening Simone and even little Tracy—"

So they were. Simone was still barking and Tracy had clapped both hands over her eyes. As for Laurie, the spectacle of gorgeous Leo Rampkin behaving like a ruffian and a cad, resorting to violence as a means of achieving his end in an argument was an earth-shaking discovery. She was seeing him with fresh, new eyes. And not liking what she saw at all.

In the midst of all the general uproar, the doorbell chimed again. Loudly and insistently, trying to knife through the clamor of the room. Again and again, the chimes tolled.

And again.

And again.

Until Laurie heard the noise and galloped to answer.

To be greeted on the doorstep by two people, one of whom was the last person in the world she wanted to see at that precise moment of her life.

The ever-loving Belle Ballantine, complete in all her well-dressed beauty, and assumed air of woman of the world.

And the tall, grey-templed, nice looking man she met at the ball game. Mr. Jimmy Perkins, ex-athlete and opportunist deluxe.

"Laurrrrrieeeeeeel" Belle Ballantine cooed in her best talking-to-another-female voice. "How marvelous you look, dear."

"Gee, thanks," Laurie snapped. "Hi, Mr. Perkins. Come on in. You're just in time."

Jimmy Perkins looked astounded. He half-smiled.

"I am? For what may I ask?"

"Mister Kinkaid is all set to throw out the first ball. And its name is Leo Rampkin," Laurie Partridge said with deep satisfaction.

"I don't know anybody named Kinkaid," Jimmy Perkins grinned at her sharp wit, "but I do know Leo Rampkin and this I gotta see. Come on, young lady"—he took Belle Ballantine by the elbow—"looks like they're having some kind of party inside and we're just in time. As long as we arrived at the same time, we might as well see it together. After you."

Laurie turned and walked back into the house.

A bewildered Belle Ballantine, her entrance ruined, allowed herself to be led by Jimmy Perkins into the interior of Partridge House. Belle was perplexed to her oh, so white teeth.

From which came sounds that were definitely not musical.

Both from the direction of the living room.

And Belle Ballantine's throat.

13

WELCOME HOME, KEITH

☐ In the end, it was beautiful.

Shirley Partridge could not have worked things out better if she had employed the genius of a Machiavelli or the greatest minds in the Pentagon. She had done the right thing; she had not pushed Keith Partridge into a decision nor had she tried to influence him above and beyond the provinces of motherhood. A boy's best friend may be his mother but there are some things a boy must find out for himself.

The greatest thing that could have happened to Keith was the small matter of his injuring his thumb in a ball game. A thumb he needed to fulfill his role as anchor man for the Partridge Family in their night club act. So that made it all too easy for him to make his final judgment and decision. And hadn't Reuben Kinkaid said it all? And so beautifully, too?

Yes, it all worked out for the best. Fitting and proper all the way.

And right in that crowded living room of the house with everybody standing around to watch it and remember it and understand the beauty of it. A boy sticking to his last and making the right decision, based on the wonderful, grand feeling of family unity and love. At first, it seemed like there was going to be nothing but a fight. What with Reuben and Leo Rampkin doing a dance around the room, squaring off, but then the tension broke when Laurie came marching back from the front foyer with Belle Ballantine and Jimmy Perkins in tow. The fight stopped.

Perkins, with the instinct of a manager, had cooled the would-be gladiators off, then talked to Keith and in a moment of very quiet wonder, with Belle Ballantine too dazed to make like a vamp and Leo Rampkin suddenly looking less than a hero, Keith Partridge had summed up all his feelings. Everybody had listened, the kids, too, with Simone staring glassily from beneath the long, low sofa and in that very special moment, Shirley Partridge admired her son above all the men in the world. His father, had he been alive to hear, would have been very proud of him. Shirley was proud enough for both of them.

Sitting on his rehearsal stool, the electric guitar across his knees, Keith had held up his bad thumb for all of them to see and said the words that would ring in his mother's heart and mind forever.

It was as beautiful as anything Shirley had ever read by Keats or Shelley. Or *anybody!*

". . . thanks for the offer, Mr. Perkins. You, too, Leo . . . but I've decided to remain a member of the Partridge Family. You see, I *am* a pretty good musician and I owe some kind of responsibility to my mother and the kids. Heck, maybe I could be a good ballplayer, maybe not. Who knows? I could have been just lucky last Saturday at the Fair and again on Monday night. Anyway—it's not a hard decision for me to make. I know I can play this guitar and carry a tune. I'm not so sure I could be a day-in, day-out ballplayer. I'll admit for awhile there I thought I could. And it . . . would be nice . . . but look how I let *this* team down . . ." He was holding up the thumb and indicating his brothers and sisters who were all hanging onto his every word in almost stunned silence. "They counted on me to play the Twilight Room with them. And play my best. I wasn't thinking of them when I played those ball games. I was being very selfish. I didn't do it on purpose but I should have remembered. A musician needs his hands, too. Just like a ballplayer. Now, thanks to my foolish ego, we'll be minus one guitar at the Twilight Room. This thumb won't be ready for two weeks. But I'll tell you this: I'm going to sing my head off in that Room and maybe play the best four-fingered guitar anybody ever heard. And that's why I'm going to stay with the Family and be

118

what I was cut out to be. A guitar player and a member of the family. I owe nothing less to my brothers and sisters. And my mother. Without whom, I would never have had any choice to make at all. And that's all I got to say right now."

The silence after those words was long and memorable.

And then there was an absolute flurry of bodies and expressions of varying sentiments hurled at Keith from all sides.

Reuben Kinkaid, to his own great surprise, blew his nose noisily and reached for a handkerchief. Keith shook his head and stared down at his offending thumb as if he wanted to cut it off, if he could. Shirley Partridge, meanwhile, had come forward to crush him in her arms. He had spoken like the man he was definitely growing up to be. And she was so proud of him. She couldn't have said how proud. But Keith could see for himself.

Jimmy Perkins made his goodbyes and Keith walked him to the door of the house, anxious to get away from his mother, who was capable of making him cry like a baby when she got that tender look on her face. She looked at him that way every time he got sick or he did something that she liked very much.

At the door, in the still hot sunlight that clutched Meadowville in a clammy vise, Perkins shook hands with Keith. With the good right hand. Keith managed a theatrical wince.

"At least it's the left hand, Mr. Perkins. I'll be all right with my good hand."

"Take care, son. You're doing the right thing. I still think you'd make a heck of a ballplayer. If you change your mind next year, call me, huh?"

"You got a deal." Keith grinned. "Must be great being a ballplayer at that."

Jimmy Perkins winked.

"Try it sometime and see."

"I just might at that. Some day."

"So long, Keith. You sure can hit a baseball."

"Thanks, sir."

"Well—"

Jimmy Perkins waved goodbye and walked down the driveway, glancing at his watch. He still had enough time to catch the two o'clock train out of Meadowville and to reflect long and hard on boys who could hit baseballs as if they were born to do nothing else giving it all up for playing the guitar. Well, win a couple, lose a couple. For a manager, there is no other philosophy or yardstick of accomplishment. Jimmy Perkins had already dismissed Leo Rampkin without a second thought. The opportunists of this world have to take care of themselves. Jimmy Perkins had already made his last farewell to Meadowville and the budding boy wonder, Keith Partridge.

Laurie Partridge closed her books on Leo Rampkin without a look back. The mad passion which had begun from afar with a glamorous male crossing her range of interest had all fizzled in the living room when she saw him being ugly with Reuben Kinkaid. Now, as she dismissed him and Belle Ballantine from her view of the world, everything seemed much sunnier in Meadowville that day. Let Belle Ballantine have him! She, Laurie Partridge, no longer *wanted* him.

Therein lay the all-important difference.

Glumly, Leo Rampkin muttered his goodbyes to Shirley Partridge and Keith and the kids and Reuben Kinkaid snorted and turned his back on him to busy himself with something or other in the black leather attache case. Leo gritted his teeth and moved out of the room. Lost, with no one paying any attention to her at all, a considerably deflated Belle Ballantine trailed helplessly after him. Leo didn't even look back once. From her advantageous position on the living room steps, Laurie jauntily waved goodbye. She was feeling just fine.

He had to pass Laurie on his way out so Leo paused to mumble something. Laurie arched her eyebrows and entirely for Belle Ballantine's edification, said haughtily:

"Did you say something, Mr. Rampkin?"

"Laurie, I—"

"*Yesssssss?*"

Laurie was milking it for all it was worth. The moment, the triumph, the letting Belle *know* that she was no longer interested in Leo Rampkin and that she, Belle, could have him. All six feet of him!

Leo Rampkin put his teeth together and gritted out a "See you around!" and stomped in defeat from the living room. Belle Ballantine tried a superior smile that didn't come off, then simply ducked her head and ran after him. When the front door slammed, Laurie Partridge brushed her palms together in exquisite self-satisfaction.

The moment had been sweet. Not bitter-sweet, at all.

She really hadn't given a darn!

And the knowledge of that made her feel simply marvelous.

Life did have its compensating triumphs, small as they were!

Christopher, Danny and Tracy were all crowding around Keith now that he had come back into the room. Danny was patting him on the back and uttering words of wisdom, medical opinion and the salutary effects of making one's own decisions. He sounded just like Reuben Kinkaid doing it. So much so that Reuben looked up from the attache case and scowled. The familiar Kinkaid scowl; the one that got deals done.

"Hey, kid. Stop shyster-lawyering, will you? That's my department."

"So what, Mister Kinkaid?" Danny offered. "I can always say you taught me all I know."

Reuben Kinkaid sighed in defeat.

"You always have the topper, don't you, Danny?"

Danny Partridge grinned, his freckles blooming.

"Uh huh," he said.

Now, with the living room once more restored to some sort of order, Shirley Partridge gazed for a moment around the room and counted her blessings. In order. Keith, a son to be proud of with his thumb and all; Laurie, a daughter who could make up her own mind, too; and Danny, who was growing by leaps and bounds into the teenage world; and Christopher and Tracy, still little children, but all too lovable and just as vulnerable and just as strong, in their own way, as all the others. Five formidable Partridges.

Two guitars, one set of drums, a tambourine and five singing voices. And her own talents to add to the Partridge stew. To simmer and boil and bubble over with all the love in the world.

And Reuben Kinkaid.

A manager—and a friend—in a million.

Ready to come running at the first sign of trouble. Ready to pitch in, advise, help—ready even to fight if necessary!

Yes, Life wasn't so bad if you had all those things going for you. All those dependable, wonderful things.

As Shirley Partridge most very definitely had.

Before she could lapse into a moony mood of love and happiness, Keith Partridge suddenly leaped onto his rehearsal stool, swept up the guitar, putting it across his lap with the one good hand he had left and sang out: "Hey! The Twilight Room, remember? Let's get this rehearsal on the road!"

Simone ran around the room as Christopher thumped his drums and Tracy rattled her tambourine. Quickly, Laurie and Danny joined Keith on the makeshift bandstand. Everybody was bouncing.

Shirley Partridge stood up before them and Reuben Kinkaid sat back on the sofa to watch, his harried face for once settling into a relaxed aspect. Even Reuben looked happy with the way things had turned out. Shirley picked up her wooden baton and waved it in mock musicianship. Sternly and with great theatricality.

"Okay, Partridge Family," Shirley Partridge sang out with a buoyant delight, "From the top. *Eyes For You I Have* . . . a-one, a-two, a-three . . ."

The Partridge Family swung into their song.

And the living room rocked with music.

And the love that can only come from mutual talents fused in a unified segment of *sharing*.

Sharing the best and the worst that life has to offer.

Shirley Partridge had learned the great secret a very long time ago. A secret which was not occult so much as plain and very self-evident. But it was a secret which gave much in return if you didn't keep it a secret from the people you cared the most about.

Which was:

A very little love can go a very long way.

A very great deal of love can stretch from here to Infinity.

With or without music.

14

CONSIDER YOURSELF

□ "He is!"

"He isn't!"

"He is so!"

"He is not!"

"Ah, Laurie, you're a dum-dum!"

"So are you, Keith Partridge!"

"Children, please—"

"Mom, make him stop calling Foster Kendall a square. Just because he cuts his hair short, reads good books—"

"Big deal! I read good books, too, but I'm no square!"

"Keith, please stop picking on your sister. If she likes Foster Kendall, that's her business, not yours. Nor will I tolerate all this noise and confusion on our first day off in weeks. And Tracy, please pick up your doll. Don't leave it in the middle of the room like that where everybody can walk all over it. Christopher! Will you stop biting your nails—!"

Everything was back to normal. All too soon.

The Twilight Room had been a sensational engagement. SRO crowds, enthusiastic audiences, great reviews in *Variety* and the accommodations in the combination club-hotel had been simply fantastic. And here it was, the second week, and already the Partridges were having their usual minor tiffs. Laurie had already discovered the cocktail pianist in the bar lounge, a lanky, studious genius named Foster Kendall, and Keith was razzing her about it. Keith's thumb had gone back down to normal size and nobody had noticed his four-finger playing the first week of the engagement. Also, his normal older-brother syndrome had returned. Needling Laurie about her taste in men and all her frequent uses of the word *relevant* for everything she liked. Foster Kendall, of course, was very *relevant* indeed but to Keith, anybody who approved of the Vietnamese War was a big drip of high order. Not that Laurie approved but she did find Foster Kendall's views fascinating.

As for Danny, he had gone back to studying *The Wall Street Journal*, which Reuben Kinkaid managed to send him daily to keep him happy. After all, anything to help a budding Wall Street titan.

Tracy, of course, kept up with her dolls, buying new ones all the time. Christopher's nail-biting was a very recent phenomenon and Shirley intended to keep her eyes on that development. After all, musicians should not bite their nails, let alone star drummers in band acts!

But, all in all, everything was going very well indeed. Keith never even turned to the sport pages to follow the baseball results. It was as if he had shut the door on that part of his life forever. The Partridges were all sailing very smoothly indeed and Reuben Kinkaid had already arranged the open dates when they could record their albums for the Emko people.

It was turning into another justly profitable, successful year for the act known as the Partridge Family.

And then came the cherry atop the cream pie.

Reuben Kinkaid called long distance from Hollywood, California and Shirley took the call in her bedroom. All the kids were out of the room on various personal errands. Only scruffy Simone, sleepy and content, lay on Shirley's lap, sleeping the sleep of all happy dogs everywhere. Dogs who never have to go off to hunt for bones.

"Shirley? Reuben Kinkaid here."

"Hi, Reuben. What are you doing in sunny Cal?"

His chuckle was almost a purr of self-congratulation.

"That's got you interested, has it? Good. How are the kids?"

"Never better. Keith's got his old thumb back, practically. But give, Reuben. What are you doing in Hollywood?"

"Shirley, I am a genius. You know that, don't you?"

"Never doubted it for a minute, Mister Kinkaid."

"And I never have steered you wrong, have I?"

"Never. But I'm going to count to three and if you don't cut out all this mystery, I'm going to hang up. I promised myself a beauty sleep this afternoon while the kids were out—"

"You don't need it," he interrupted gallantly, "because you're beautiful enough for two women already. All right, Mrs. Partridge, here it is. They're making a movie out here. A big, old-time, as-they-used-to-make-them extravaganza. With Gene Kelly and Ginger Rogers. And guess what? They want the Partridge Family for a ten-minute segment. I'll give you five seconds to digest the information and then you may thank me. Very warmly and very gratefully."

The news hit her like a blow to the pulse.

"Reuben—that's marvelous! You're not clowning around—"

"Who me?" he protested. "I don't make jokes long distance. And not when it's the biggest thing that's happened to us yet. You dig, girl? The Silver Screen! Hollywood! With a cast of thousands! And an audience of millions—"

Long after he had hung up, sounding self-pleased and happier than she had ever known him to be, sleep was out of the question. She fidgeted so much she even woke Simone up, who growled with annoyance and slunk off to a quiet corner of the room. Shirley could not contain herself. She could barely wait for the kids to return from their errands. It was very hard to hold back the news, as they all drifted back into the hotel suite, almost one by one. Finally, they were all present and Shirley gathered them together in the big outside room to make her announcement. She stared at all their expectant, curious faces before she launched into her big surprise—Reuben Kinkaid's surprise, really—and then quietly and very proudly she told them.

In short concise sentences.

She wasn't exactly prepared for the ho-hums and apathy that greeted her wonderful news.

Keith yawned and scratched himself on the left ear.

"Hollywood, huh? Not bad."

Danny changed the subject, of all things.

"Can we have lobster for supper, Mom? They had a great red one in the club window when we came in."

"Did Foster Kendall call while I was out?" Laurie asked, her eyes glowing. Tracy and Christopher had straggled into the bedroom, looking tired and beat.

"Uh—no—" Shirley said, stricken almost speechless by her

unimpressed siblings. Confused, she looked at the remaining three Partridges in the room. "Didn't you hear what I said? We're all going to be in the movies!"

Keith and Laurie and Danny all exchanged looks. They managed to seem extremely baffled by their mother's attitude.

"Uh huh," Keith said. "Hollywood. We heard you."

"It's nice to be in the movies at last," Danny agreed, "but we still haven't appeared on the Dick Cavett Show."

"Yes," Laurie offered. "After all, Hollywood was bound to get around to us sooner or later—"

Dazed, Shirley Partridge watched them all repair to their separate corners of the room. Almost meekly, she sat down and stared at the far wall of the room where a reproduction of a Chagall painting dominated the decor. Within her mind, her thoughts rioted. And then she had to smile. It wasn't a Generation Gap, she wasn't getting any older nor was it the jaded talk of young people who had become stars all too soon. In their formative years.

No, it was none of that.

It was simply an eternal verity that time, tide and circumstance would never change. The Partridge Family was a big-time act, a headline act, but for all of that, its members, excluding herself, were nothing more complex than human beings. Nothing less simple than little people, growing up.

Keith and Laurie and Danny and Christopher and Tracy were still nothing more than *children*. For all their sophistication.

And to children, all things are possible.

Even *Hollywood!*

Why should Hollywood be so unusual to them?

It was just another place, after all.

Like New York, Las Vegas, San Francisco. Or Meadowville.

Later on, Laurie wandered over to Shirley Partridge's chair and kissed her suddenly on the cheek. Shirley stirred, in surprise.

"What was that for, young lady?"

"Oh, nothing."

"Nothing? Come on, now. You kiss me out of a clear blue sky, it can't be for nothing. What's up?"

"Oh, Mom! Sometimes you're such a square!"

"Meaning?"

126

"Meaning I just love you, you dope," Laurie Partridge said, laughing her way into the next room.

Shirley Partridge remained where she was in her chair. But her heart beat a little faster and her blood raced a little more joyously in her veins.

Yessirree, no matter what happened, the Partridge Family could always be counted on for a few little surprises.

Like a declaration of love out of a clear blue sky.

Or a plain ordinary hotel room.

Humming happily to herself, Shirley Partridge rose from the chair to change into her costume for that night's performance at the Twilight Room. Simone was now sound asleep under the chair close to the door of the suite.

Keith called out from the next room.

"Hey, Mom!"

"Yes, Keith?"

"Do I get a raise in salary when I hit eighteen?"

She smiled, calling back. "Is it important to you?"

"Nope. Just asking."

"Then ask me when you're eighteen, will you? I got a lot of other things on my mind right now."

"Sure, Mom."

She reached for the red dress and cute weskit on the hanger by her bed and little Tracy suddenly toddled into view, clutching her by now very ragged doll, which was at least five years old.

"Mom, I got a problem."

"You have, Tracy? Tell me about it."

"My doll's getting very old and if she gets sick and dies, what do we do with her? I mean—can we give her a funeral?"

Shirley crouched and hugged Tracy Partridge to her bosom. Her eyes filled with tears. For a long moment, she couldn't speak.

"No, honey. We keep her. Because dollies never die. They stay with us forever and forever. Wait and see."

Tracy's eyes lit up like two beacons of joy. Her smile was radiant.

"Honest? No fooling?"

"No foolin'!" Shirley Partridge said. "She's ours forever."

And so was love.

FIRST TIME EVER
IN PAPERBACK

OTHER CURTIS
TV TITLES
AVAILABLE

CURTIS
BOOKS
